Ravenous Snakes

ONYX GOLD

CAYÉLLE
HAZE
PUBLISHING

Ravenous Snakes

Copyright © 2021 by Onyx Gold

This book is a work of fiction. Names, characters, places, and incidents are the product of the author's imagination or are used fictitiously. Any resemblance to actual events, locales, or persons, living or dead, is coincidental.

All rights reserved. No part of this publication may be reproduced, distributed, or transmitted in any form or by any means, including photocopying, recording, or other electronic or mechanical methods, without the prior written permission of the publisher, except in the case of brief quotations embodied in critical reviews and certain other noncommercial uses permitted by copyright law.

For permission requests, contact the publisher below:

Cayélle Publishing/Haze Imprint
Lancaster, California USA
www.CayellePublishing.com

Orders by U.S. trade bookstores and wholesalers, please contact Freadom Distribution:
Tel: (833) 229-3553 ext 813 or email: Freadom@Cayelle.com

Categories: 1. Romance 2. Crime/Thriller 3. Suspense
Printed in the United States of America

Cover Art by Robin Ludwig Design, Inc.
Interior Design & Typesetting by Ampersand Book Interiors
Library of Congress Control Number 2021935676

ISBN: 978-1-952404-20-7 [paperback]
ISBN: 978-1-952404-21-4 [ebook]

Contents

Prologue

Fter glowing warm kisses, Zia remembered to open the mail she'd been clutching. Bryce returned to assist Jazz with hanging the grand opening sign for Fairfield Fink Literary Law Firm's grand opening.

The mysterious white envelope had all her attention. She'd stopped receiving mail in her maiden name over six months ago, so she was significantly intrigued that it was addressed to Zia Lennox. Wondering what it could be, she tore it open and removed the paper clipped photographs with attached note.

"This one's on the house. I'm sorry. – Kevin."

She flipped through the photos and gasped.

Her heart exploded and her nerves scattered at the sight of the various images of Bryce and Jazz, meeting up with each other, holding hands, kissing, in bed together.

Her heart shattered inside her chest as she viewed more images of Jazz conversing with Amahle and Bryce having a meal with Baxter. She covered her mouth with her hand. The dozens of scattered images meshed together, creating an aching vision before her eyes as she viewed the rest.

She recalled Bryce taking the confession of her affair with such loving ease. His extraordinary ability to abstain from premarital sex made so much more sense now. Jazmine never being in a relationship with any men or women — no dates, no ex-boyfriends, no stories. How she and Bryce would always peculiarly be unreachable at the same time.

The pounding of her broken heart was interrupted by a barking Bugs, her very best friend. Bugs jumped up and down in the air, anxious and worried because he'd felt her emotions dip. The baby kicked as the images continued to weave together inside her mind — painting an eerily vivid picture.

The South African couple spewing all of that garbage about ancient Yorubian royalty was for Baxter's sake. If he truly believed she was Eve in the flesh, he would've trust her. Amahle and Kungawo knew exactly what to say to Baxter because Jazz had told them. Once Baxter fell victim to that rehearsed script without thinking twice, he let his guard down and slept without imprisoning her inside of his arms.

The only reason Baxter never killed Bryce was because they were a team. The files on that flash drive were never meant to convict Baxter and Detective Barnes was a pawn. Jazmine, as Dwight's daughter, was the only woman who was safe from him, until Zia came along. Once she came into the picture, she'd become a threat to Jazz's inheritance because Zia had replaced her as the only woman he wouldn't kill. Now Zia's convinced he wouldn't have ever hurt her.

Baxter never sent that blackmail packet!

Bryce and Jazmine clearly wanted to merge Weingart and Paradigm long ago, but Dwight was standing in the way. Jazz wanted her inheritance and Bryce wanted his. Zia was used to help them both achieve their goal. With the joining of the two powerhouses, they can effectively corner every market and no one could stop them. Together, they're now the two wealthiest and most powerful people in the United States.

Zia's the only loose end left.

Her hands trembled and her stomach twisted into constrictor knots as she turned to face them.

Chapter ONE

LIKE A LIT CIGARETTE, ZIA'S COMBUSTIBLE GLARE threatens to burn a hole right through the back of Jazmine's backstabbing head. Difficult for her smile to appear genuine since she'd discovered the truth about her so-called best friend. For the sake of her unborn child, her performance has been award-winning, as of late.

Each morning she performs her hygienic rituals while repeating the same line to herself as a reminder. *Lights, camera, action!*

Zia stands outside of the main conference room, near the bannister, peering down at Jazz, longing for the moment when she's able to confront her. Wanting nothing more than to end her, the way she'd ended her own father.

How many times had Jazz lied? How many times was she pinned underneath Zia's husband as Zia struggled with her guilt, seeking Jazmine's guidance and support?

The very thought repulses her beyond belief.

Her nostrils flare.

"Mrs. Fink?" the administrative assistant calls.

Snapping out of her murderous trance, she turns.

"Yes."

"The client is becoming anxious. They insist the meeting —"

"I'll be right in."

She'll handle the meeting solo, since Jazmine's swollen ego forbids her from actually doing any work. Zia rolls her eyes, rubs her protruding belly, and enters the conference room.

With her shoulders pulled back, she breezes through it without missing a beat, all while enduring their facetious banter. She secures the client and the contract before swiftly exiting, allowing the clerical staff to clean up.

She drives away from Fairfield Fink Literary Law Firm (FFL) without notifying anyone. She owns thirty-three and a third of it, which makes her a boss just as much as Bryce and Jazmine. She's grown tired of playing secretary just because they have more money. If they can goof off during the work day without informing her, then she'll leave when she damn well pleases. She's extremely annoyed with everyone and everything. She's sleepy, hungry, and her back is aching.

She all but burns rubber as she skids into her driveway, seething. Her hands grip the steering wheel so tight they go numb. Her nerves curl into pretzel knots. She craves the Xan, but she cannot have it. She can't even have caffeine. Slowly counting backwards from twenty, she inhales and exhales until her limbs stop shaking, and her tensions unravel.

She releases her tightly wound fingers, allowing the blood to circulate. Glancing up at the mini mansion Bryce built for them, she swallows her anger and tries to let it all go. Once more, and then again as she pulls into the garage.

She believes Bryce deserves her forgiveness while Jazmine does not because she'd never lied to her. Jazmine did all of the lying. When she'd turned to her mother for advice, she received wisdom and truth her anger didn't want.

"Baby, you're focusing your anger on Jazmine because you desire Bryce. You can't hate one without hating the other because they both have wronged you," her mother had said.

She angrily turns her cell phone off before exiting the car and slamming the door, grateful to be home where she can drop the façade and openly despise their betrayal, without controlling her facial expressions. Within seconds of walking inside, Bugs dashes through his doggie door, bringing her first smile of the day.

She misses being able to bend to scoop him up. She leans sideways to scratch him behind his ears — her dearest friend in this whole wide screwed up world. She grabs his previously prepared meal from the fridge and pops it into the microwave.

Her highly perceptive pal jumps onto the nearest chair so he can reach her belly just when her oversensitive emotions swell. Tears moisten her lids as she allows him to bark at his unborn friend. He's become more protective lately. The most telling part is that he despises Jazmine.

After feeding Bugs, she waddles up the stairs into the bedroom, kicks off her flats, and lays backwards on the bed, fully dressed. She regrets it because it's a struggle to get up from that position.

Her body sinks into the cloud-like mattress and she relaxes. Bugs jumps onto the bed and rests his chin on her lap. He either gobbled his meal swiftly or he'd rather be up here with her. It's amazing that something now exists in this world more important to him than his food. It's laughable and adorable.

Zia allows her cement lids to close. Her thoughts scatter among the random. She falls asleep with her arms cradling her baby boy. She dreamt his name was Damien.

"Mommy can't wait to hold you, Damien."

THE SMELL OF FRESH BREAD BAKING ROUSES HER FROM HER vampiric slumber. Her lids flutter open and her senses slowly return her to the present. Laughter echos from downstairs. She accidentally tries to sit completely upright.

"Youch."

How many times must she forget her belly reaches her thighs now? She rolls over onto her side, scoots her body towards the edge of the bed, and pushes herself up by leaning on the nightstand. She waddles over to the doorway and sticks her head out.

She hisses and smacks her lips when she hears Jazmine's voice.

"Doesn't she have somewhere else to be?"

She carefully descends the hardwood staircase, keeping one hand on the bannister. When she enters the kitchen, she notices Jazmine's wearing her favorite apron. Zia pauses, then turns around to fix her face. It gets harder and harder every day.

"She's awake!" Jazmine squeals in phony delight as she rushes over to hug Zia.

Zia reluctantly returns the embrace. Bugs growls at her. Zia grins at him. *Good boy.* Over her shoulder, Bryce beams their way while stirring a pot of boiling food on the stove. Jazmine rubs Zia's stomach.

Zia inwardly cringes, but doesn't flinch.

"How'd you sleep? Are you hungry?"

"I'm always hungry."

Bryce hands the wooden spoon to Jazmine.

"Don't let that burn," he tells her before wrapping his arms around his heavily pregnant wife.

He kisses Zia's forehead. She manages a smirk as he massages Damien's temporary home.

"How are you feeling?"

"Are you asking me or Damien?"

"You know we haven't decided on that name."

"I know, I know. I just … I like it."

"Well, I'm asking you how you're feeling. There's no him without you."

"I'm fine."

"I figured you'd be hungry when you woke up."

Yeah, but he didn't need Jazmine's help to cook the meal. Zia walks toward the fridge, beyond annoyed. She grabs some crisp green grapes and a bottle of water.

"How many glasses of milk have you had today?"

"Babe, I've had 4 already." She's in no mood to be chastised with that witch around.

"Then you'll have a glass with dinner?"

She nods while shoving her mouth. Being six months pregnant allows her to keep her mouth occupied fifty-percent of the time. Lately, she's been afraid of what might come out of it. She cuts her eyes at Jazmine, who catches it this time.

"Oh, I hope it's okay that I borrowed your apron." She unties the straps.

"No, no. It's fine. I just miss the days when it would fit around my waist."

"You'll be back to your teeny tiny self in no time."

"Mm mmm, I like her like this." Bryce hugs her from behind, kissing her neck.

It sends electrifying chills down her spine. He hasn't touched her intimately since her second trimester, reasoning he doesn't want to hurt the baby, even though the doctor has told him repeatedly he won't.

Zia's more inclined to believe he's taken up residency inside someone else's body. The very wicked witch cooking dinner in her damn house right now. As far as Zia knows, there's rat poison in it. Maybe the only reason why she's still breathing is because of Damien.

Zia opts out of the scene. She grabs more snacks from the fridge.

"I'll be upstairs."

"Dinner will be ready in a bit."

"Mm hmm."

She climbs the stairs with Bugs on her heels, resolving she won't be eating any of whatever they're cooking. She'd rather starve. She needs to occupy her thoughts before she sets that bitch on fire.

She retreats into her office down the hall from the bedroom and closes the door. She prefers to spend her time there for two main reasons; the super comfy chair Bryce special ordered for her and the solitude.

An extra added bonus is that it's directly across the hall from the nursery she visits daily. This is her own little nook of the house and she'll be damned if she allows the sourness of Jazmine's betrayal to befoul it.

She powers up the PC and settles into her comfy chair. All of the previous tabs Zia had been browsing through are still open. She starts systematically reading and replying to all of the company emails. Then she checks her finances. Her eyes bulged slightly at seeing her nest egg nearing $1oo million. Bryce has been in charge of her finances since they married and Zia doesn't even know the specifics of how he managed to grow it so much. She doesn't want that on her plate right now, deciding to wait until after Damien is born.

She returns her attention to work, reviewing several new contracts. She sometimes finds herself missing the grind of securing clientele from the front line. She enjoyed it because of the excitement of being the first person to read an awesome story before it became the new world-wide sensation. Even though she misses the thrill of her old job, she realizes an executive position is much more aligned with all of her experience. She's seen too many great stories get rejected on a ridiculous basis, such as politics, laziness, or venomous decisions disguised as ethical dilemmas.

She doesn't want to live to see herself become a corporate stale Gale's by allowing herself to get too comfortable, though it is much safer. She makes time to read queries, partials, and even fulls after they've been vetted. Her emails are now heavily filtered, so there aren't as many exciting things for her to read anymore. Though it helps with her anxiety and stress quite a bit, some part of her yearns for adventure.

After a while she toggles over to her personal email tab. The dryness of her inbox depresses her. After the whole Dwight Fairfield scandal-tragedy hit the news, almost everyone she knew, and even people she didn't know, had their own opinion about her, so she changed her email address and deleted all social media. Without her presence on the net, society moved on to the next person to judge and crucify. The emails and letters eventually stopped.

She leans further back in her comfy chair and sighs, responding to order messages quickly. She clicks on her junk folder, which is relatively new. Just when she hovers the mouse over the empty button, one particular email warrants a further look. A single sentence in the preview stops her dead in her tracks.

"He may be gone, but his will be done. How well did you know him?"

Her heart raced as she clicked to open the email. She had received opinionated emails before. This was different. Zia wanted to believe this was just another opinionated stranger who knew nothing about her or Baxter, but the email carried an eerie undertone that wouldn't allow her to press the delete button. Instead, she was compelled to press reply.

"Get a life! Law enforcement tracks these emails by the way. Unless you want to go to jail, I suggest you leave me alone."

She typed ferociously, slamming her fingers against the keyboard. She sent the response without giving it a second thought. Then she blocked the sender, created a special filter to send all their emails to the trash bin. She's so frazzled, she forgets to sign out and power down the laptop.

She hastily pushed herself up off the chair, letting her big belly lead the way. She stretched until her joints popped. A sigh of relief escaped her lips, but her hands were trembling. She waddled into the nursery for a bit of calming scenery.

The reinforced oak crib is centered in the room, away from the walls and windows. Books and stuffed animals adorn the shelves. She fiddles with attachment hanging over the crib. The moon and stars swirl in the air above the crib, hypnotizing her. A wave of calm relief rushes through her. The neutral tones soothe and comfort her until her tremors subside.

Feeling lighter on her feet and happier, Zia leaves the nursery and walks toward the bedroom. Jazmine's annoying giggles float up from downstairs, rousing her anger once again.

"She needs to go home."

She stomps down the hallway, preparing to demand that Jazmine go home at once. Bryce appears near the top of the stairs, startling her. He immediately cradles her belly near his face. He glances up at her fur-rowed brow, but continues rubbing and massaging Zia's belly, waiting for her face to relax.

"I'll bring our food upstairs and send Jazmine home."

A huge burden falls off her back.

He takes one more step up, until he is face to face with Zia, and kisses her. Their lips press together softly as Bryce caresses her face and tucks a tuft of her boisterous curly hair behind her left ear.

She was grateful she didn't have to be the bad guy. However, his actions confirm that he is aware of the tension between her and her former friend, so he shouldn't continue inviting her over. She wants her peace when she's home and Jazmine is no longer part of that.

She smiled lovingly at Bryce before retreating down the hall. His footsteps trail off down the stairs as turns the lights off in the nursery and then the study. She was so preoccupied with thoughts of permanently removing Jazmine from her life, she failed to notice the new email notification on her computer screen. She slammed it closed.

"Jazmine needs to be permanently gone," she thought. "No more fake smiles. No more lingering. No more using the business as an excuse. I want her gone. Just gone!"

HIS FINGERS GLIDED SENSUOUSLY ACROSS THE ILLUMINATED computer screen, wishing it was her glowing flesh instead. Oh, how he wished he could feel the lush flutter of her full ebony lashes. It didn't matter that she was tainted. He was angry and resentful that she was with child, but she was not yet beyond redemption or correction. His mentor had trained him well on the many ways to make anew what had been defiled.

The best thing that could've happened to him was the demise of his beloved master. He would often wonder how long he could deny his own desires in order to faithfully serve another. Now that his master is no longer around, and he is no longer bound by those chains, he can implement all the plans he'd been holding onto.

He turned and gazed across the dimly lit lab. The supply kept from the FDA inspection sat behind reinforced glass at the other end of the room. Having been forewarned about the inspection, all he had to do was move it. All the accusations have since evaporated and become nothing but a pool of meaningless conspiracy theories. Personally, he never cared for the medical plan because it was flawed. He had voiced his hesitation to Dwight just once. The man's wrath kept him from ever speaking out against him again.

He had found Zia. He always wanted Zia and deserved her. He is in love with her and she is in love with him too. She just doesn't know it.

Chapter TWO

Bryce and Zia went out shopping for groceries while they discussed her upcoming business flight to Nebraska. Bryce didn't even want to consider her travel plans at all until she agreed to take the Weingart jet.

"Just in case," he'd said.

She was sympathetic to his concerns for her and the baby, so she agreed.

Zia isn't the biggest fan of grocery shopping, not since her belly got so big. Walking around just made her back and feet ache. She used the cart to use as a walker, so Bryce had to get his own to put the groceries in. She didn't want to push around a full cart, but buying less made for more trips.

"We should start using a nifty app for our grocery needs, don't you think?" Bryce suggested.

"Genius. Can we start now so I can get the heck out of here?" she chuckled.

"I'll finish up. You can go rest in the car." He kissed her forehead.

"You sure?"

"Absolutely."

"This better not be another ploy to hire a maid."

"Haha. Not that we couldn't use one, but I'll settle for the app."

She smiled and nodded before going back to the car. The radio played nonsensical music on a low volume while the air conditioning was on full blast. It was mid-spring, so not very hot outside, but Zia was boiling.

She was sweating and out of breath.

"God, if this is what it takes to bake another human, I'm only signing up for one round. Whew!"

Once the air in the car turned chilly, she shut the radio off and fished her phone from her purse. Work was always able to distract her. She lazily scrolled through her notifications with her thumb while fanning air towards her face with her free hand.

A person email notification perked her up. She smiled, believing it to be her mother or her assistant, Jenn, sending her more baby purchase links. Her smile evaporated when she read the subject.

"You think you knew Baxter/Dwight, think again!"

Was it from the same stalker who emailed her the other night? Just those few words captivated her completely. She knew Baxter was a liar, so the email didn't tell her anything new, but the fact that someone was going out of their way bothered her.

The tip of her finger hovered over the delete button. She was torn between deleting and replying. She knew that reading the rest of the email would open up a bag of snakes, and she really didn't need any further complications in her life. She decided to delete it.

Before she clicked that button, she noticed the email had an attachment. That pulled and poked at her mind even more. There were too many unknowns to ignore because it could very well be a picture or video of her and Baxter in the throes of passion. She couldn't fight against her curiosity any longer, so she opened it.

She ignored the text and went straight for the attachment. It was a photo. She hesitated for a moment but then clicked on the download button. It seemed like ages, waiting for it to download, but eventually it did and she opened it.

The image was fuzzy and old. She had to lean in close to her screen and squint. There were two young men standing next to each other. They looked around 12-years-old in the photo. They both looked similar to each other and very familiar. She was sure she had seen at least one of

their faces before. She stared at the picture, waiting for her brain to prop-
agate. All of a sudden, it hit her like a soccer ball to the face.

She knew the boy in the photo, but she couldn't believe there were two
of them. There couldn't be two of them. It isn't possible. The two boys
in the photo, there was no doubt in her mind they resembled a young
Baxter, but … Her jaw dropped as she stared. It had to be fake. She just
wasn't willing to believe there were two Baxters. Wouldn't Jazmine have
known her father was a twin?

Her face flushed red and her blood bubbled. She was filled with rage
and it was just enough to overpower her confusion. Her anger took over
her, she clicked on the reply button, and viciously typed with her thumbs,
all the while growling and panting, because this was nonsense.

*"What are you trying to pull here? Do you really think I'm dumb
enough to fall for photoshop? Nice try, but I'm reporting you to
the police if you don't go away!"*

She didn't waste a second before clicking on send.

Zia marked the email as spam and locked her phone before tossing it
onto the car's dashboard. She leaned back further just to get away from
it. She turned the radio on full blast and allowed the music to deafen her
to the world. She glared out the window and kept an eye out for Bryce.
Surely, he would be back soon, but she can never ever tell him her former
lover might've been a twin. Just no.

ZIA HAS BEEN AVOIDING HER PC FOR THE PAST FEW DAYS.
Every time she went on to look at her emails, she saw more of them from
the mysterious cyber stalker. All of them with tempting and taunting
details in the subject line. All of them tugging and pulling at her curiosity.

"You'll want to see this."
"Calling the police is a bad idea."
"Ever wondered how he really found you?"

Zia managed to ignore each one of them, but it was only getting harder. She might be able to stop herself from opening up the emails, but she couldn't stop her mind from wondering. She couldn't stop thinking about them; she couldn't stop thinking about that photo. She kept thinking the truth she once sought could lie with the cyber-stalker.

Bryce was downstairs making the two of them dinner while she sat in the nursery, trying to calm herself. It was hard not to think about the unopened emails, when her PC was in the next room. She tried to think of anything else but the knowledge kept worming its way through her thoughts. It just wouldn't go away. She needed to get to the bottom of it before it raised her blood pressure. The only way she'd gain relief was by reading them.

She stomped out of the nursery and snatched her hibernating laptop screen open. Her full attention was fixed on the emails. She opened up her email and shuffled through the spam, looking for one of the many emails she had put in there. She hoped that not all of them had been automatically deleted yet.

She gasped when she finally found one. It was there now, right in front of her, and suddenly she didn't want to open it anymore. All of the horrible and wicked things it could be came to her mind. She had to overcome that though. There was no choice but to open the email now and it seemed like such an easy thing to do. All she had to do was click one button. It couldn't be anything more ridiculous than the picture in the last email. As if she were in a trance, she moved the mouse to the open button and clicked it.

She read the text again in an effort to delay downloading the file attached. It read:

"Sometimes, it's the smallest details that are important."

She read it over and over expecting to find some kind of hidden message. Eventually she gave up on that idea and scrolled down to the attachment. It was a video. She hesitated but clicked the download button. Her PC was faster than her phone and it downloaded the video instantly.

She opened it up and prayed it wasn't something else to drive her crazy. The video was of poor quality and black and white. She decided that it must be video footage from some street camera. The camera was pointed at some kind of restaurant or café, she didn't recognize which one.

She watched for a while but nothing particularly interesting happened. Then she saw two faces that she recognized. Her stomach churned and she felt sick as Bryce escorted Jazz to a table right in front of the camera. She rolled her eyes and sighed. She already knew about all this, the pictures she received from Kevin already let her know that Bryce and Jazz were fooling around behind her back. Whoever this stalker is he needs to catch up and stop spreading old news.

She was ready to close the video before it made her throw up, but then something dawned on her. The email said that the small details are important. Maybe she was right. Maybe there is a secret message there. She scanned every inch of the screen looking for something in the video, something that stood out. Perhaps there was something there that the sender of the email actually wanted her to see. Just when she thought that there was nothing there besides Bryce and Jazz having a romantic meal, out of the corner of her eye she spotted a number at the bottom of the video.

Zia felt her heart fall to the pit of her stomach. She couldn't believe it but the truth is right in front of her. The video was dated at least two years before Zia had even met Bryce. She figured they started messing around after Bryce and Zia had a relationship but this video showed that not only did they know each other before, but that they were in a relationship before Zia even knew Bryce existed. Things were clicking into place and Zia started thinking about just how long this plan of theirs was in place.

She felt so angry she didn't know what to do. She felt like throwing something against the wall, but at the same time she was scared. She was overwhelmed with anger and confusion all at the same time.

She forced herself to delete the video and turn off her PC. What she had just witnessed was so crazy it had to be fake. She couldn't bring herself to believe it but she also couldn't allow herself to stay in the dark while people made plans around her.

Bryce called for her from downstairs. Dinner must be ready but she has all but lost her appetite. Still, she couldn't hide up here all night long. She put on the face she had been working on ever since finding out about Jazz's betrayal. She ate dinner with Bryce and they even watched a movie before going to bed. She did her best to hide how she was really feeling.

That night, Zia woke up in a sweat. She had nightmare after nightmare. Each nightmare was different and frightening but somehow familiar. They were like long-forgotten memories twisted into a monstrous horror story.

She had dreams about Baxter, only there were two of them. The one Baxter was sweet, loving, and kind. The other Baxter was like a cold, dark beast, growling and hissing at her every thought and move. One second she would be with the sweet Baxter and the next second the beast of Baxter would emerge and attack her.

She had dreams about Bryce, only it wasn't really him. It would look and act like him but the moment she turned her back to him, whatever it was, its head would begin to spin around to reveal a twisted version of Bryce on the other side. This Bryce almost didn't look human. It would laugh, revealing rows of sharp teeth and lean forward to bite her.

After she woke up the dreams seemed to fade away. Her memory of them was transparent and the only solid thing left behind was the way they made her feel. They made her feel unsafe and betrayed. She felt as if the walls were closing in on her and everyone she knew was hiding something behind their backs.

Bryce was still sleeping soundly next to her. She watched him for a moment. The rise and fall of his chest was calming for her. He wasn't a snorer, but his breathing was deep enough to resemble a soft snore. Watching Bryce sleep seemed to soothe and relax her. That feeling didn't last very long though. The feeling she had when she was asleep came creeping back into her mind and she could no longer look at Bryce without seeing the monster he was in her dreams.

She lay back in the bed and allowed the heavy lids of her eyes to slowly close. She remained still and waited for sleep to take over her. She wasn't sure when she finally fell asleep, she only remembers having more nightmares. Somehow the nightmares seemed more like old memories, twisted

and dark versions of them.

WHEN ZIA WOKE UP, THE BED BESIDE HER WAS EMPTY AND the heavy curtains were still drawn closed. She sat up as much as she could to glance at the alarm clock on Bryce's side of the bed. It was nearly one. She slid her legs off the bed one leg at a time and stretched. Her back was aching and her feet were sore, but that was nothing new. She put her gown on and attempted to put her slippers on, but it was a difficult task given that she couldn't see her feet or the floor in front of them. Eventually she gave up and decided to deal with the cold floor. Suddenly her stomach growled at her and she had so many cravings.

She came out of the room and rushed down the stairs as fast as she could without falling over. She raided the kitchen cupboards and fridge for any snack she could eat that didn't require cooking or preparation. She found a few packets of chips, a jar of peanut butter, and a jar of pickles in the fridge. Suddenly the taste of pickles dipped into peanut butter seemed like a really good idea to her. She grabbed all of the snacks and put them in one of the shopping bags, so she could safely and easily carry them all upstairs with her.

Before she headed back up the stairs, she prepared some food for Bugs and placed his bowl on the floor. It was difficult to lean over and place the bowl down so she just ended up dropping it on the floor. He came rushing in from some other part of the house the moment his bowl touched the floor.

"Good boy," Zia whispered as she grabbed her snacks and headed back up the stairs.

Her lack of sleep didn't mean she didn't have to work. She headed into her office and ate her snacks while going through her emails. Work was boring, but eating made it more enjoyable. She did this until late afternoon when she heard the key in the door letting her know that Bryce was home. It was only at this point that she realized Bryce wasn't in the house and she hadn't even noticed. She saw that he wasn't in bed when she woke up but he didn't leave a note or a message letting her know he would be gone. She was so preoccupied with eating and getting those horrible nightmares off her mind that Bryce was the last thing on her mind.

It seemed a shame to leave her comfortable chair but she did so anyway and met Bryce at the top of the staircase.

"Hey babe," Bryce said with a smile. "Have you been drinking your milk today?"

Zia saw Bryce's face and images from her nightmares flashed through her mind. She forced a smile and a nod.

"Where were you?" she asked him. "You just disappeared without a note or a message. That's very unlike you."

"I needed to head into the office for a work emergency," Bryce replied. His eyes were wide as if Zia's question shocked him. "I just woke up this morning and left, I didn't want to wake you and I didn't leave a note because I honestly thought you'd still be asleep by the time I got back. I'm sorry, did I worry you?"

Zia didn't want to distrust Bryce, but something about his reaction to her question raised a red flag for her. She was done ignoring red flags. *"If this so-called 'work emergency' has anything to do with Jazz,"* she thought.

"What was the emergency?" She asked, trying to sound as uninterested as possible.

"I just left some files in the office that I needed to go through before Monday," Bryce replied.

Zia stared at him for a while. He answered so quickly and smoothly that she was sure he was telling the truth. Thinking that he might be lying to her formed a knot in her stomach and made her feel sick. Those dreams and the emails must be making her paranoid.

"I'm sorry," she sighed, "I guess I was worried."

Zia put her hand on her belly and Bryce placed his hand beside hers. He stepped close and their foreheads touched ever so gently.

"Now that you're moving forward with the pregnancy, we should think about getting you some help," he suggested. "We can get you a personal assistant that can live in the house and stay home with you. You'll feel safer when I'm not here."

"Sounds a lot like a nanny for adults," Zia chuckled. "I think that's a good idea."

"I'll go make us some lunch," Bryce gave her a kiss and walked back down the stairs.

Zia didn't want to tell him that she had already been snacking for most of the afternoon because she was still hungry and wanted whatever Bryce was making. She went back to her office to turn off her PC, but before she could, she saw that she had received a new email. She didn't think twice about it and opened it. She gasped as she realized it was another one from that stalker written in the exact same tone, but that wasn't what made her gasp.

"Don't tell me you believed the 'work emergency' excuse. That's the oldest trick in the book."

Zia's blood froze in her veins and a painful shiver shot down her spine. She wasn't sure what frightened her more. The fact that whoever was writing the email was feeding into her suspicions that Bryce was lying, or that this stalker seems to be able to hear their conversations as they're happening. She began to feel like she did a year ago when Jazz had told her Baxter might have bugged her home. Maybe it was happening again.

"Zia, food is almost ready," Bryce called from downstairs. "Come down and we can watch a movie or something while we eat."

Zia had to compose herself. Her head was spinning and her world was slowly crumbling around her. It did occur to her to show him the emails but that would only make things worse. A small part of her wanted to see more. A small part of her trusted the emails more than Bryce. There were too many questions that needed to be answered, even if all of this was just one big joke and the video and picture were fake. She needed to see where this was all going.

She closed everything, turned off her PC, and headed downstairs where Bryce was waiting for her. She had to once again put on a face and pretend everything is okay. *"Lights, camera, action,"* she thought to herself as she made her way down the stairs.

THAT NIGHT ZIA HAD EVEN MORE NIGHTMARES, EACH ONE more horrible than the last. They seemed so real to her. It was as if she was reliving old, forgotten memories. At the same time they were so unbelievable she just couldn't allow herself to think that they were true.

After another sleepless night she decided it was time to visit her therapist. She hadn't gone to see her in a few years but desperate times call for desperate measures. The lack of sleep couldn't be good for the baby after all. Besides, all these nightmares only left her with questions to ask. Questions that needed answering.

Zia got out of bed early, making sure not to wake Bryce, and called her therapist's office. She made an appointment for later on in the day. Then she sat down and thought of a lie to tell Bryce. She obviously couldn't allow him to find out about the dreams, and if he knew she was going to talk to a therapist then he would want to know why. If he knew about the dreams he would ask too many questions. Zia had too many questions of her own that needed to be answered and she didn't want Bryce to stand in her way of those answers.

As if she was being sent a sign from God, she got a message on her phone. She checked it. It was from Jenn. She was recently hired as a lit agent at FFLL. Zia can't remember the last time she spoke to Jenn but she remembers having a great time with her at the wedding. She opened and read the message:

> "Hey Zee, long time no see. I made a rhyme, don't know if you noticed. Was wondering if you wanted to meet up for coffee or something today? Can be like old times at Fargo Towers in the cafeteria."

Zia smiled genuinely. She felt bad for seeing Jenn as a way to lie to Bryce about going to the therapist. At the same time, she needed this and it was an opportunity she wasn't going to let pass by. She quickly typed a reply to Jenn with a time and a place to meet up. It was her favorite café and it was close to her therapist's office. She gave herself enough time to visit her therapist before meeting up with her. Then she made herself some breakfast and waited for Bryce to wake up.

When Bryce finally woke up she waited for him to make his breakfast and they had a normal conversation. Then she mentioned that she made plans with Jenn later. She tried to make it sound like they were old plans and she had forgotten until today. Bryce was a bit surprised but he didn't ask too many questions about it. When it was time for her to go he escorted her to the car.

"Be safe," Bryce told her as she turned on the engine.

He leaned through the window and reached to put her seatbelt on. He clicked it into place and kissed her. She leaned her forehead against his and held it there for a moment. It felt nice, warm and safe. Zia would love to stay right here for just a little longer but there were other, more pressing matters to attend to. If she didn't leave now she would be late for her appointment.

She leaned away from Bryce and put the car in gear. Bryce watched her drive away and Zia's heart broke just a little. How could it be that easy? How could she lie to him like that, as if it was only water off of a hippo's back? She had lied to him before, back when she was with Baxter, but back then it was eating away at her until she couldn't lie any longer. It felt easier to lie now. Bryce had lied to her as well after all, and she had a video and photos to prove it. How could she be sure that he wasn't still lying to her and doing things behind her back?

"Did he even go to the office yesterday?" She thought to herself. "What if he was doing something else? What if he was with her?" She decided there was no reason for her to feel bad about lying to him. Everyone lies. There's no harm in it. There was no way for her to know if Bryce is being truthful, or even faithful to her. Bryce could have been with Jazz yesterday and not at the office for all she knew. Why shouldn't she lie to get her way when everyone else does it? It was only a small lie after all.

SHE MADE IT TO HER THERAPIST'S OFFICE IN TIME FOR HER appointment, even though all the traffic lights on the way there acted as if they wanted her to be late. She parked the car and rushed into the building. Rushing for a pregnant lady is basically just a quick waddle. Once she got to the reception area they escorted her straight into the office where her therapist was waiting.

Zia told her therapist about the nightmares and how they make her feel. She explained them in as much detail as she could manage without bringing back the horrible memories. More importantly she told the therapist how they didn't seem like nightmares at all. She told her how they almost seemed like memories or warnings. As if something inside her was trying to tell her something she was missing. She felt as though the nightmares were twisted memories of something important that she had either forgotten or blocked out.

"Well that's highly possible," the therapist said, putting her notebook that she had been writing in the whole time down. "You see, often when people have gone through a traumatic experience as you have, they block out memories that might remind them of that experience. Sometimes these are big and important memories and other times they are small things that don't really mean that much."

"These memories seem as though they are only about small things but I feel like they matter," Zia insisted.

The therapist thought about it for a moment and picked her notebook up again. She went through a few pages before she spoke again.

"In that case, these could be small details that are a part of a bigger picture. They seem as though they aren't that important until they're pieced together with this bigger picture. Then the puzzle starts to make sense and you see something that you were missing."

Zia leaned forward in her seat, "Do you think that's what these nightmares are?"

"Unfortunately that is not my field of expertise, but I will say that it is a possibility." She flipped to a new page in the notebook, scribbled something down, and pulled the page out. "All I can do now is direct you to someone who knows more about this than I do." She leaned over and handed the piece of paper to Zia. "Perhaps he can help you figure out what these dreams really mean."

Zia glanced down at the piece of paper. It had a name and a number on it but before she could pay too much attention to it she caught sight of the time. If she didn't leave now she would be late for her meeting with Jenn.

She thanked the therapist, put the piece of paper in her purse and rushed back to her car. She had already dealt with the payment when they started. Making sure the charge was taken directly from Zia's account in a way that Bryce wouldn't notice.

JENN STOOD ON THE CORNER OF THE STREET OUTSIDE THE café waiting. Zia drove up and quickly found a parking spot. When you're pregnant no one questions where you park. She struggled out of the car, dropping her purse on the floor and growling at it like a dog. Jenn rushed over and picked up the purse for her.

Jenn's jaw was halfway to the floor and her eyes were popping out of her head as she handed Zia her purse.

"Oh my god Zia, you ate the moon!"

"That's hilarious Jenn, you won't be making jokes like that when you're pregnant, everything hurts, and suddenly pickles and peanut butter doesn't make you want to throw up."

They stared at each other for a moment then burst out in laughter. Jenn wrapped her arms around Zia gently and hugged her. Zia was more than happy to hug back. They walked into the café and grabbed a seat near the window so they could look out at the street.

Zia couldn't remember the last time she could just sit and enjoy speaking to people like this. She was surprised how she didn't feel scared or anxious. They were surrounded by people but she didn't care because she knew that none of them would come sit by her or try to talk to her. It was just her and Jenn.

Zia remembered the days she used to meet Jenn and Jazz for lunch in the cafeteria in Fargo Tower. Those days seemed like they were part of the distant past. They were long gone and they weren't coming back. Zia would never be able to sit down with Jazz again. The fact that Jenn was reminding her of Jazz was bad enough but she could at least stomach that.

Back then even when Jenn or other people were sitting at the table it was still just Zia and Jazz. They held the conversation. Others might talk but they never really listened; they were in their own world. Now that Zia was actually talking with Jenn it was different.

They laughed as they talked about old times and how glad they both were to be rid of Spark. Zia asked Jenn how her new position at FFLL was going.

"It's amazing!" Jenn yelled a little too loudly drawing attention from the rest of the café for a brief moment. "This job makes what I was doing at Spark look like slave work. They people are nicer too, although I rarely speak with anyone."

"You rarely speak with anyone?" Zia giggled. "I find that hard to believe, you're such a social butterfly."

"Yes I am, and proud of it! Watch me flutter my social butterfly wings." Jenn spread her arms out and flapped them about for a moment.

Zia couldn't contain her laughter and it burst out louder than she wanted it to. All of a sudden every eye in the café turned to see one woman waving her arms in the air while a pregnant lady doubled over laughing.

"Jenn stop it."

Jenn sat back down and gasped, grabbing Zia's arm. "Have you planned a baby shower yet? You have to plan a baby shower. Oh, please let me plan the baby shower!"

Zia hesitated to answer.

"Oh wait, I guess Jazz has probably already started planning it hasn't she." She let go of Zia's arm and the excitement left her eyes.

The idea of having a baby shower made Zia cringe, but the idea of Jazz planning it made her want to throw up in her mouth.

"Jazz hasn't started planning anything," Zia said. "Why don't you plan my baby shower? I know you'll make it an amazing one."

Jenn's eyes lit up like a Christmas tree and a smile spread across her face from one ear to the other. She jumped up and down in her seat and thanked Zia about a hundred times before the beverages they ordered finally arrived. They spent the rest of the day discussing plans for the baby shower and other plans for the baby. Zia found herself feeling comfortable and enjoying herself. She always knew what a fun person Jenn was but she never knew how much they would actually get along if she put some effort in. After Jazz's betrayal, Zia was in the market for a new friend.

AFTER HER MEETING WITH JENN, ZIA HEADED STRAIGHT home. She was floating and glowing. She had a good day and she was convinced that nothing could spoil her mood. At least that's what she thought until she walked through the door to see Jazz and Bryce dancing in the kitchen again.

"Oh hey babe," Bryce said as she walked in. "Welcome home!"

He rushed over and gave her a gentle hug by wrapping his arms around her neck and keeping his body as far away from the baby as possible. He kissed her and then bent down and pressed his cheek against her belly.

Zia smiled down at Bryce but when she glanced up at Jazz, she felt like her head would burst from all the anger. She kept smiling through the anger.

"Hey Zee, how was your day?" Jazz asked with her same innocent and loyal smile.

Her smile was probably more fake than Zia's.

"It was good. I really enjoyed seeing Jenn after all this time."

"Jenn?" Jazz seemed surprised but Zia detected a hint of anger as well. "You went to see Jenn?"

Zia saw this as an opportunity to get under Jazz's skin. She saw it as a small taste of revenge.

"Yes, I met her for coffee. I didn't have coffee though, because of the baby, I just had tea. Jenn was great though. She is really enjoying her new job but we still spoke about those good ol' days at Fargo Tower." Zia was an actress that deserved to win an Oscar. All she could think about was the best way to make Jazz as angry as possible. "Oh, and Jenn offered to plan my baby shower so I told her she could. We discussed plans for it and everything."

"You told Jenn she could plan the baby shower?" Jazz couldn't hold back her jealousy any longer. "You told me you weren't going to have a baby shower. I should be the one planning the baby shower. I'm your best friend!"

Both Zia and Bryce were shocked by her outburst. Although Zia was shocked, she was also pleased with herself for a job well done. She did a good job at hiding the devious smile threatening to spread across her face. Instead she replaced it with an open mouth, raised eyebrows, and bulging eyes.

"Calm down Jazz, I didn't think it would bother you that much. It's just a baby shower." Zia was so proud of herself. "It's too late now. I already told Jenn she could plan it and I'm not about to tell her that she can't. That wouldn't be fair to her."

Bryce kept his distance from the girls and he kept his mouth shut. He didn't want to see them fight but he also knew he would only make it worse if he got involved.

"Well, I guess it doesn't matter," Jazz shrugged it off. "Jenn will probably come to me for help anyway. She's not that good at planning things."

"She seemed like she had it all figured out to me. I think she's going to plan a great baby shower. Don't you Bryce?"

Zia didn't like the fact that Bryce was staying out of it. She didn't want him to stay neutral. She wanted him to choose a side, his wife's side, her side.

Bryce froze like a deer in headlights, with both girls staring at him and each one waiting for him to pick a side.

"It's just a baby shower," he chuckled. "Does it really matter who gets to plan it? I'm sure Jenn will do just as good a job as Jazz would have done."

Both women rolled their eyes and turned away from him. He managed to find an answer that annoyed both Jazz and Zia.

"Well, I wish all the best luck to her new friend," Jazz said as she gathered her bag. "Planning things is hard, I hope she can handle it." She glanced at the clock. "Unfortunately I have to get going. Goodbye Bryce, thank you for the awesome day." She gave him a hug and Zia felt today's lunch force its way up her throat. Then she turned to Zia. "Goodbye Zee!"

Jazz came forward and tried to give her a hug but Bugs appeared in front of Zia and growled at her. Jazz retreated from the hug and smiled down at Bugs.

"Good boy," she muttered before making her way to the door.

For the rest of the night Bryce and Zia didn't speak much. They ate dinner and then Bryce went into his office to do some work. Zia powered up her PC to do some work but she made an effort to avoid looking at her emails. She didn't want this good day to be ended by another strange email from that stalker. She decided to go into the room and empty her purse before getting ready for bed.

She found the piece of paper her therapist had given her and she read it. It was the name Dr. Herb Gardner and a number to call beneath it. She picked up her phone and researched the name quickly. He is a hypnotist.

"Why would she want me to see a hypnotist?"

Bryce walked into the room and she quickly crumpled up the paper and put it inside her purse.

"Getting ready for bed without me?" He asked. "Don't you want me to help you undress and get into your gown?"

Zia smiled at Bryce and threw her purse to the floor. Bryce undressed her slowly and left at least one kiss on each limb. Then he gently slipped her gown on and helped her get into bed. He then undressed himself, put on some boxers, and slid in next to her.

Zia sat in the bed with a thought in her mind. This thought wasn't a new one but it only just popped up in her mind now. She'd been wanting to talk to Bryce about it for a while and after the way Jazz acted today she couldn't think of a better time to bring it up.

"I think we should buy Jazz out of the company," she blurted.

Chapter
THREE

Z IA SILENTLY MADE HERSELF SOME EGGS, BACON, AND toast for breakfast. She didn't want to wake Bryce who was sleeping on the couch in the next room. He went to go sleep on the couch after their fight last night. It was the first time they hadn't slept in the same bed in over a year.

She yawned while waiting for the toast to pop out of the toaster. She hadn't gotten much sleep. How could she sleep knowing that Bryce was so angry with her that he couldn't even be in the same room? She still doesn't understand why he blew up at her like that. All she did was suggest that they try buying Jazz's shares of FFLL, which would effectively get her out of the company. She didn't expect Bryce would freak out.

The toast popped up and she grabbed it quickly. She was worried the sound may have woken Bryce up but some part of her didn't care if it did. She was angry at him, even if she didn't show it last night when he was yelling at her. She was the one that sat there calm and quiet. She was the one that kept her composure. As far as she is concerned she is the one with the moral high ground.

Bryce walked into the room just as she finished spreading butter and jam on her toast. She glanced at him out of the corner of her eye but she didn't fully look up at him. He stood on the side of the kitchen in a T-shirt and boxers, staring at her.

"You should have asked me to make you breakfast," Bryce said.

"You were asleep," Zia mumbled while she carried her breakfast tray over to the fridge. She opened up the fridge and pulled out the milk. "I have to pack for my flight later today so I couldn't wait until you woke up." Zia made a point to be cold when she talked to him.

Bryce sighed, "Can we talk about this. I don't like the feeling of you flying off to another city later while we're in a fight."

"We're not in a fight." Zia poured herself a glass of milk. "If I recall correctly the fight ended last night when you decided to sleep on the couch instead of in bed with me." She picked up the breakfast tray and headed towards the stairs.

"Zia—"

"If you wanted to talk about this Bryce then you should have done it last night. You shouldn't have run away leaving me in an empty bed. I wanted to discuss it last night. I don't want to discuss it now." She started climbing the stairs, doing her best not to look like she needed help, even though she couldn't see where she was putting her feet or hold on to the railing. "You made it clear last night how you felt about buying Jazz out of the company, so don't worry about it anymore."

"Zia, please let me explain my actions last night," Bryce insisted but he didn't follow her up the stairs.

Zia sighed, "After I'm done packing."

"Would you like me to help?"

"No, thank you, I'll be fine."

Zia made it to the top of the stairs and disappeared into the bedroom. She placed the tray down on the bed and collapsed next to it. She felt bad for being so cold to Bryce. Then she thought that he deserved it for all he had done. She couldn't help but think the only reason he freaked out about her wanting to buy Jazz out of the company is because he has feelings for her. That must be the reason. He deserved her cold shoulder.

She ate her breakfast, although she didn't enjoy it. Her mother always told her never to cook when she was angry because the food will taste of what you put in it. Zia tasted hatred and anger. She forced most of it down so she had enough energy to pack. Bryce had made plans for the private jet to take her to Nebraska later this evening. That way she would be able to sleep on the plane and land sometime in the late morning.

Zia managed to pack everything easily. Her packing skills weren't as tidy and elegant as they used to be. She didn't bother folding everything and placing it neatly in the suitcase. Instead she left the suitcase on the floor because when she tried to lift it up onto the bed it didn't go so well. Then she grabbed an item to pack, realized she couldn't bend down far enough, and ended up dropping it down into the suitcase. When the suitcase was full, she realized she couldn't bend down to close it. She didn't feel like calling Bryce to close it so she left it for now. Bryce could close it later when he helped her pack it into the car.

She finished packing earlier than she expected to, so she decided to get some work done and put some things in order before her trip. She also just wanted to sit in her comfy chair. The PC powered up quickly and she got straight into it. She sorted out emails, replied to some emails she had received a few days ago, and printed out a few things for Bryce to look at later. She was on a roll. It felt good to do work like this. It made her feel like she did in the old days when she still had to sort through that slush pile.

She decided to manually delete all the emails she had received from her stalker. She had marked them as spam but that meant they only get deleted after a certain amount of time. She had a bad feeling in her stomach that would only go away once the last email was moved to the trash bin. Maybe then the nightmares would go away. She was convinced the only reason she didn't have a nightmare last night was because she couldn't get to sleep at all.

She had done it. She clicked the delete button on the last email and a feeling of freedom swept over her, but it was short lived. Her PC made a soft clicking noise indicating she had received a new email. She clicked on the notification pop-up, which was a big mistake because it didn't just take her to the email, it opened it. She inhaled deeply. It was as if the stalker was watching her and he refused to let her get rid of him that easily. She had time to close the email but her curiosity was still too strong for her to ignore.

"I bet Bryce never told you this. What else is he hiding from you?"

Zia clicked on the file attached to the email to download it. It looked like a document but when she opened it she realized it was only a fragment of a document, not even a full page. One part of it was highlighted in yellow and circled in red. It was a bit obvious which part she was supposed to read.

She read the paragraph over and over again to understand it, but it seemed like gibberish until she realized what document it was from. It was from Bryce's inheritance. The paragraph stated how Bryce's inheritance is predicated on the consummation of his marriage to her. It goes on to explain that Bryce must produce an heir to Weingart in order to come into his full inheritance.

It didn't seem like that big a secret to Zia at first but then she thought about it. Why wouldn't Bryce tell her about it? Why would he keep something like that a secret unless he was worried about something? Zia began to think that this stalker was right. If Bryce was hiding something as simple as this from her then what else could he be hiding?

Before she could finish her thought she received another email. She clicked on the notification pop-up and the email opened. There wasn't a photo, video, or document attached to this email, it was just a short message.

"Do you feel used yet?"

THE BED ON THE WEINGART JET WAS A LOT MORE COMFORTable than Zia was expecting it to be. After she boarded the flight, saying goodbye to Bryce, she sat down for takeoff. Once they were in the air she was allowed to move around. She ordered a glass of water from the waitress and headed straight to bed. She had a long day and there was a lot on her mind. She was looking forward to a good night's sleep but she wasn't looking forward to the nightmares.

She was woken up and asked to sit in a chair with a seatbelt before they landed the next morning. There was a black BMW waiting for her when the jet landed. Her luggage was packed into the trunk for her and the waitress was kind enough to help her down the stairs of the jet. Zia had been married to Bryce and dealing with her new wealthy lifestyle for more than a year now, but it was still strange having people do things for you.

"Where to ma'am?" The driver asked her once she was inside the car, he had a southern twang in his voice just like Bryce, but not as strong.

"To the hotel first please, so I can freshen up before my meeting this afternoon," Zia replied with a smile. "I assume Bryce already sorted out a hotel for me."

The driver nodded at her through the rearview mirror and returned the smile, "Yes ma'am, I've got the hotel details right here," he passed a folder back to her. "We should be at the hotel in an hour or so."

"Thank you," Zia began unpacking the folder. "What is your name?"

"It's Rodney, ma'am."

"Thank you very much, Rodney." Never let it be said that in all her wealth Zia had forgotten her manners.

They reached the hotel in an hour just like Rodney had said. It was a grand one, with a red carpet extending out from the huge double glass door entrance, and everything seemed to have gold trimming. Someone opened the door for her, unloaded her luggage for her, and escorted her to the front desk. Rodney told her he would be back to pick her up for her meeting before driving off.

Inside the hotel the floors were made of marble tiles that were so clean that they perfectly reflected the ceiling. Crystal chandeliers hung from the ceiling and the roof had that same gold trim she saw on the outside of the building. There were lavish, leather couches to her left and shiny metal elevators to her right. She was led straight down the middle of the lobby towards the front desk. The person standing behind the desk held his head up with pride and stuck his nose out in front of him. Zia could already see how snotty he would be.

"Mrs. Fink? Uh, yes we've been expecting you." the man asked and answered himself before Zia could say anything. "Here is your key, and someone will escort you up to your room and your bags will be brought up shortly after you."

Zia took the key from him and smiled. She wanted to say thank you but the man had already turned and started talking to someone else. She made a note to mess with him later.

"This way Mrs. Fink," she heard a soft, young voice say.

She turned around to see a young man in the same uniform as the man behind the desk. This man looked no older than 16, but she figured he just had a youthful face.

"If you would follow me this way to your room," he said and started walking toward the elevators.

He led her to her room on the 30th floor and walked with her through the long hallways until they found her door. She was sure she would have gotten lost without him. She thanked him and gave him a tip before entering her room. Her luggage arrived a few minutes after her and the men were helpful enough to unpack her things onto the bed and pack the suitcase away for her. When they left she packed her things into the cupboards and drawers, then she had a quick shower and got ready for her meeting.

The room was just as bright and lavish as the hotel lobby. Zia didn't even want to imagine how much this hotel was costing her and Bryce. She decided to have a talk with him about spending money like this. She didn't need to stay in places like this, even though they're not exactly struggling with money doesn't mean they have to throw it around like this.

Rodney was there to pick her up just like he said he would be. Zia liked Rodney. Her meeting was in Valentine, Nebraska and her hotel is in Omaha.

"It's more than a five-hour drive ma'am," Rodney told her as she buckled her seat belt. "I've stocked the back of the car with drinks and snacks so just help yourself if you get hungry." Then he turned the engine on and they were off.

Zia liked Rodney even more now. The drive to the meeting would take them more than five hours but it was only taking place at the end of the work day so she was sure she would make it in time. They didn't have to stop for lunch now. Zia had eaten a quick breakfast at the hotel but she decided to dig into the snacks Rodney packed for her now. She munched on the chips, chocolates, and cookies the whole drive there and even had a short nap.

"We've arrived ma'am," Rodney's soothing southern voice woke her from her nap. "Would you like me to escort you into the building?"

Zia yawned and rubbed the sleep from her eyes before glancing out the slightly tinted window. The building in front of her reminded her of Fargo Tower. It was tall and made from boring grey brick. This was the place. There was a company inside the building that's interested in signing on FFLL as their legal party. Zia, being the charming person she is, is supposed to seal the deal, and bring papers back home for Bryce to look over and sign.

"No need for that Rodney," Zia said. "I'm sure I'll be fine from here."

"I'll wait in the car for you then ma'am. Good luck."

Zia thanked Rodney and stepped out of the car. She dusted the cookie and chip crumbs off her clothes then headed into the building. She stood tall and had pride in her step. She missed the days where she could wear heels that clicked on the floor and announced her arrival. Heels can help make an entrance. Her comfy, slip-on sneakers will have to do for now.

The front desk told her which floor to go to and pointed out the elevator for her. She got to the right floor and saw the legal team Bryce had sent waiting for her. Bryce made sure she didn't have to read or sign any documents herself because she wouldn't know what to look for. All Zia was there for was to smile and be the face of the FFLL. She was grateful for that at least, because it was the easiest job ever and Bryce was too busy at home to be able to come here himself.

Zia didn't recognize all of the people sitting there but she was sure that not all of them were part of the legal team sent by Bryce.

"Would you like my seat?"

Zia gasped and turned her head in the direction of the voice. The man standing up in front of her was tall and handsome beyond belief. He was at least three feet taller than her. His body was lean and fit but not overly muscular. There was only a hint of muscle pushing through his tightly fitted black suit. The sight of him made Zia's heart pound in her chest.

He stepped away from the chair he was sitting on and gestured for

Zia to sit down.

"Oh, thank you," Zia said, realizing that she was pregnant and it's natural for a man to offer a pregnant woman his seat.

She sat down as gracefully as she could manage and he stood beside her. They both waited in an awkward silence. She kept glancing up at him out of the corner of her eye. He was almost too handsome for words. His skin was pale, his eyes were a deep blue, and his lips were perfect. His chiseled chin gave away that he wasn't as slim as he looked at first glance. There were definitely some defined muscles underneath that clean suit and crisp white shirt.

"I'm Willem by the way," the stranger spoke so suddenly that Zia nearly jumped out of her chair. His heavy, thick British accent was a fresh sound to her ears.

"I'm Zee, I mean Zia," she stuttered. She took a few breaths to try and compose herself before she spoke again. "It's nice to meet gentlemen like you."

"True gentlemen are few and far between these days, as are beautiful and exotic women," he mused as he smiled down at her with a devilish spark in his eyes. "I try to do my best to make up for the lack of gentlemen in this world, and I see you're making up for the lack of beauty as well."

Zia's cheeks felt hot and she hoped they weren't the shining red she imagined they were. She looked down just in case they were. She had received compliments before but none were delivered with that type of elegance and with that accent.

"Are you here for the meeting?" She asked in an attempt to change the subject.

"I am here for a meeting but I'm afraid it's not the same meeting that you're here for."

Zia was relieved to hear that. That meant he doesn't work for FFLL and this may be the only time she is going to see him.

"By any chance, is your full name Zia Lennox?"

Zia looked up with her eyes wide and gasped at hearing that name. How did he know? How could he possibly know her maiden name? She would have shrugged it off if he had asked her if her last name was

Fink, ever since the merger of Paradigm and Weingart everyone knew that name, but how could he possibly guess what her maiden name was.

"You are the same literary agent that is responsible for publishing the Chiseled Bone series, am I correct?"

Zia breathed a sigh of relief. She never thought she would ever be relieved to hear about those books again, but it was better than what she was thinking.

"Yes that was me," she replied. "I actually go by Zia Fink now." She gestured to her wedding ring.

"Oh, may I offer my congratulations." He bowed forward and kissed her gently on the back of her hand.

Thankfully the doors opened and Zia and her team were called into the meeting room before he could see her blush. Zia got up to follow the rest of the team in.

"Goodbye Zia Fink," Willem called to her. "I hope we have the pleasure of meeting again."

The meeting doors closed behind Zia and she thought that'd probably be the last she'd ever see him. She was glad she'd been working on keeping her anxiety under control this past year. If not, she might have fainted or started hyperventilating the moment he smiled at her.

THE MEETING LASTED LONG BUT ZIA DIDN'T NEED TO DO anything. She just sat there, exchanged some polite smiles and a few compliments, but that was it. Then Rodney took her back to the hotel and she slept through the night. She couldn't get her mind off of that handsome stranger. Willem was intriguing to her. She wanted to know more about him but when she exited the meeting room, he was gone. She was surprised since he said he was there for a meeting but perhaps he had already finished his by the time hers was done.

Zia had the television on while she packed her suitcase once again for the flight home. She mainly had it on to distract her from her thoughts. It is natural to have thoughts of another man when you're married, but her thoughts of Willem scared her. He was new, mysterious, and perhaps a bit dangerous. He intrigued her but at the same time he reminded her of how she felt with Baxter. She didn't want that, not again. She would rather not have any man in her life.

She heard something on the television that properly distracted her. A name she was hoping she would never hear again outside of her own thoughts and nightmares. Baxter Leopold. Zia snapped her head towards the television to see a woman standing in front of the camera with the cover of Eve sitting in a box next to her head. Reaping had gone ahead with publishing the last book in the Chiseled Bone series.

Zia's legs buckled beneath her and she fell back onto the bed. He's dead, but they've brought him back. Baxter is now alive again with the publishing of Eve. She thought that she would also make money from the book sales still and that sickened her. She would never be rid of him. Baxter is dead but now he would live forever through his writing and Zia would never be able to move on and forget him.

Chapter
FOUR

ZIA JUMPED UP IN THE BED. SHE WAS SWEATING ALL over and the memories of her nightmare were already fading. It was similar to the first nightmare. Two Baxters, but one is different from the other. The curtains were closed but she could see a sliver of sunlight pushing through a gap in the middle. The sun rose on that side of the house so she knew it had to be early morning.

She had been home for several weeks now and the nightmares hadn't stopped since she learned that Reaping had gone forward with publishing Eve.

The sound of Bugs barking downstairs was at the front of her mind but that awful nightmare had left her in a dazed and confused state. She wanted to forget the whole thing but some part of her was holding on to it. She didn't want the memory of it to fade completely. Something told her it was important.

She swung her legs over the side of the bed, leaning back so she didn't put too much pressure on her protruding belly. It was only now that she noticed Bryce's side of the bed was empty. These days Bryce had been really busy with work and she hardly saw him. She had decided she would take a week's rest from her trip before heading back into work with him.

Bugs' barking banged in her head, bringing attention to the sudden headache she now had. If Bryce was awake why wasn't he doing anything about Bugs' barking? Unless he had left for work already, which meant that she was alone.

Zia managed to wiggle her way off of the bed. She slipped her gown on and attempted to put on her slippers. She remembered how hard it was just to do that with her belly now. She didn't even attempt it and instead walked around barefoot. She'd been doing that a lot lately. Her feet were cold but she ignored them as she walked towards the stairs, following Bugs' barking.

She got to the top of the staircase and saw Bugs barking by the door. Her heart jumped up into her throat. Bugs only ever did that when there was someone on the other side of the door. She was sure if someone had knocked or rang the doorbell she would have heard them, or Bryce would have answered the door already if he was still home.

She was glued to the top of the staircase with her eyes, unblinking, staring down at the front door. She waited for either Bugs to stop barking or for someone on the other side to announce themselves. The sound of her heart beating became louder than the sound of Bugs' barking.

"Bryce!" She called out. Her voice echoed through the empty house but there was no answer. "Bryce?" There was still no answer and Bugs barked even louder with some violent growls thrown in.

Zia had two options; walk down the stairs and answer the door. She could only hope that there wasn't a murderer or her stalker on the other side. The second option was to call Bugs away from the door, go back into her bedroom, and pretend none of this had happened. Zia wasn't the bravest of people, but she wasn't prepared to be one of those women who are scared of every little thing either.

She took her first step down the stairs. She held onto the railing and leaned back slightly so she could see where she was placing her feet. By the time she had taken her second step down the stairs she spotted a shadow move through the small gap at the bottom of the stairs. She froze for a split second, along with the blood inside her veins then she turned around and started climbing back up the stairs.

"Bugs!" She called, "Come here boy."

Bugs was a good little boy and he followed her up the stairs straight away. He followed her all the way into the bedroom and she closed the door behind them. She may be paranoid. She may be overacting, but she was a heavily pregnant woman at home alone, and she was sure there was someone stalking around outside her house. Why would there be someone at the front door not knocking, ringing the doorbell, or even just calling out 'is someone home?' She wasn't being paranoid, she was being careful.

Zia waited in the bedroom with Bugs by her side until Bryce could return and protect her. She wasn't sure where he was or why he would leave without telling her, or leaving a note, but she knew that she would feel a little safer once he came back. It was at that moment her stomach growled at her angrily and she all of a sudden had a craving for peanut butter and banana on toast.

She made a note that they should have a second kitchen installed upstairs for emergencies like this one. She knew Bryce would laugh at her when she told him, but at least then there should be a bar fridge and snack drawer in the bedroom.

ZIA WASN'T SURE AT WHAT POINT SHE FELL ASLEEP BUT IT was long enough to give her pins and needles in her arm. She got up slowly to see Bugs jumping up and down by the bedroom door. He wasn't barking though, and that comforted her. He was probably just hungry or he needed to use the bathroom.

She sat up in the bed for a while as sounds from downstairs traveled up. She heard soft music playing, Bryce's music. She heard the opening and closing of cupboards and drawers. Bryce must be home and in the kitchen cooking. She felt a wave of relief and security rush over her, but it was quickly replaced by annoyance and anger when she heard Jazmine's laugh.

Although she would much rather wait until Jazz left, she decided to go downstairs. She didn't want to leave the two of them alone for too long. She wondered if Bryce had even come to check on her. Did he wonder why she locked herself in the room? Was he worried at all? She thought about all this as she rolled out of the bed and unlocked the bedroom door.

Bugs rushed out in front of her and nearly tripped on his way down the stairs. She stepped out and a sweet aroma filled her nostrils. It smelt like fish and white sauce and she was reminded how hungry she was by her growling stomach. She walked to the top of the staircase and glanced over the side of the railing. She was hoping to spot either Bryce or Jazz in the kitchen. She wasn't sure what she was looking for but she wanted to see what was happening before she went down there.

A sharp pain shot straight up her spine and banged against the base of her skull. She leaned forward and grabbed hold of the railing with both hands. Her vision was black around the edges and the pain at the base of her skull built up until it covered her whole head. The world was blurry and fading away. She tried to call out for help but she didn't have the strength left in her. She saw the stairs in front of her and her legs felt weak. She was going to fall! She used whatever strength she had to walk away from the stairs. Before she knew what was happening her legs gave way and she was lying on her back.

She didn't feel herself hit the ground and she wasn't sure what was happening. Someone called out for Bryce but it wasn't her. She used whatever strength she had left to lift her head. She saw Jazz standing over her and staring down at her, and then the world went black.

Zɪᴀ's ᴇʏᴇs ᴏᴘᴇɴᴇᴅ ᴛᴏ ʙʀɪɢʜᴛ, ᴡʜɪᴛᴇ ʟɪɢʜᴛs ᴀɴᴅ ᴀ ᴄᴏɴstant but soothing beeping sound. Her muscles were stiff and every part of her hurt. She felt cold and naked and her throat was dry and sore.

The light above her was blinding so for a few minutes she just stayed still and waited for her eyes to adjust. Once they were, she turned her head slightly to look around. She was surrounded by a white curtain, hanging from a metal railing suspended above her. There were wires protruding from her arm leading to a machine beside her. She was in the hospital. Zia's eyes filled with tears as she looked down at her belly. She hoped her baby was okay.

She tried to call out for someone but her throat was too dry and only a whisper escaped through her cracked lips. She wondered how long she would have to lie here when the curtain was pulled back slightly. Bryce's face was the first thing she saw and the tears came out like a waterfall.

Bryce collapsed to his knees beside her and took her hand in his. His touch was soft and reassuring. Zia squeezed his hand but she had very little strength to do so for too long. Suddenly Zia's thoughts were overwhelmed by questions about what happened to her, and questions about the baby. Her eyes shot down to her belly once again. Her eyes were asking the question but her voice could not.

"The baby's fine," Bryce responded to the question she couldn't ask. "The doctors said that you collapsed and it was probably due to stress. They said that heavily pregnant women most of the time can't handle excitement or stress as well as they would have before they were pregnant. You just overwhelmed yourself that's all."

Zia let out a sigh and new tears escaped the corner of her eyes. These were tears of joy and relief.

"You're going to be fine," Bryce continued, "You just got a bit bruised from the fall that's all. They said you could come home after the test results come back and everything looks good."

Zia didn't know how to feel about that. She didn't want to spend any longer than she needed to in a hospital bed but she also didn't want to go back home. Her home was where she was supposed to feel safe but couldn't. She was sure that the stress that made her collapse must have come from the excitement, or rather fear, earlier in the day. There had been someone on the other side of that door. Bugs knew they were there but Zia had a feeling they didn't want her to know they were there. She couldn't feel safe there. She wasn't sure if she would feel safe alone in a hospital either.

Bryce stayed by her side for most of the day but he had to go eventually to sort some things out at work. Several people visited her throughout the day. Jenn came by to talk and confirmed that the baby shower would be put on halt until Zia was feeling up to it. When Jenn left Zia was left alone again, until an unlikely face peered around the curtain.

"Are you accepting visitors?" Willem asked, smiling down at her with his deep blue eyes.

Zia was confused but also somehow relieved to see him again. There were a lot of questions swimming through her mind. How did he know she was in the hospital? Why is he even here? Is it strange for someone you barely know and only met once to visit you in the hospital? All these questions she needed answered. For now she was just glad to see a face that she didn't hate or completely distrust.

"Willem," she said with a harsh and unused voice. "What are you doing here?"

"I understand you must be confused and even shocked to see me here, but before you go calling security I can fully explain myself," he pulled the curtain back slightly and stepped inside the security of it. "I came to L.A. for some business when I heard that the famous lit agent that is responsible for publishing Chiseled Bone lives here. I decided to come by and see you so I asked around for you. I have a lot of contacts you see, and somehow one of them heard you were admitted to hospital a few days ago. I would have come to see you straight away but I was worried I would scare you."

Zia gave him a weary but genuine smile. She couldn't believe a stranger would go through that much trouble just to see her again. He must be a really big fan. She wasn't used to lit agents getting fans. Usually the readers didn't look past the person who wrote the book.

"I … I'm flattered," Zia managed to speak before coughing and quickly reaching for the water beside her bed.

Willem jumped forward and grabbed the water before she could. She let her head fall back and her arms rest while he lifted the cup up to her lips. She looked him in the eye as she took a sip. She couldn't believe how blue they were. She felt like she was swimming in the deepest ocean whenever she looked into them.

"You don't have to speak," Willem said as he put the cup down, "I can see that it's difficult for you right now. I won't bother you for long either. I just came to see that you were okay, I'll go now and let you rest."

Willem turned and pulled the curtain back to make his exit.

"Wait," Zia tried to shout but it was only a faint whisper. Willem glanced back at her, his eyes hanging on her every word. "Thank you for coming. It was nice to see you again."

Willem smiled at her and the sight of that warm, genuine smile healed her more than any of the medicine did. He turned back to her and took her hand in his. His touch was soft and gentle like a cloud. He leaned forward and kissed her hand. Then he nodded his head slightly and left her alone once again.

Zia didn't care that she was alone. She felt so much better now after seeing him. He was a true gentleman and he really seemed to care about her. It was enough to make the butterflies flutter in her stomach, or maybe that was the baby kicking.

Chapter
FIVE

WILLEM CAME TO VISIT HER IN THE HOSPITAL MUL-tiple times during her few days there. He sat with her and they talked about books, and literature. He listed all of his favorite books to her and mentioned how most of them were published by Reaping. He explained that after discovering that almost all of his favorite books shared the same publishing house he got interested in researching who was behind the success of all those books. That's how he came to know her. She was the literary agent who was responsible for publishing two of his favorite book series.

Zia couldn't believe that someone would care that much about what went into the publication of a book. Everyone knows how books get published, but nobody actually cares about anyone but the person who wrote it. Willem was like a breath of fresh air to her.

"I'm so glad I've met someone who cares about the literary world as much as you do Willem," Zia exclaimed.

"Please, call me Lem," he insisted. "That's what my friends call me after all."

Zia enjoyed their chats and it was one of the few things that made her nights in the hospital bearable. They even exchanged numbers and when he left her alone their conversation would continue through text. He made her feel safe and secure. That was something she hadn't been able to feel in a long time. Bryce used to be her rock to hold onto in the greatest of storms, but now she was seeing him in a new light and she didn't like what he looked like.

Lem was her new rock to hold on to and she had this feeling that he was different. He was genuine. He wasn't hiding anything from her or lying to her. She never thought that she could feel this close to someone she barely knew, but she did and she liked it. She found herself lying in that bed and waiting for the time of day when he would come and visit. Even when Bryce was there, she was still waiting for the moment she would get to see Lem again.

Only two days passed and the doctors finally released Zia from the hospital. Everything was fine with her and the baby and she was allowed to go home, but Zia didn't feel like going home. She didn't feel safe there. The only thing keeping her calm was the thought of seeing Bugs again and the bouquet of flowers Willem sent her this morning.

The flowers were beautiful and elegant, just like Willem. They sat in a crystal vase that looked like it was designed by Picasso or someone aspiring to be him. It swirled, curved, and twisted in ways she didn't know a crystal vase could. It seemed unnatural but beautiful all the same. The flowers were arranged in a way where each one had room to show off its colorful blooms, and healthy leaves. No flower was the same and she didn't even recognize all of them. She knew the roses, there was one of each color. She thought she recognized a peace lily, but the rest were wild and exotic to her.

It came with a card that simply said, "Not even all the flowers in this vase can match your exotic beauty. Get well soon, Willem." Zia blushed at the card but she made sure to hide it before Bryce could see. He arrived a little after the flowers to help Zia pack and take her home.

"Who are the flowers from?" Bryce asked her as they were getting ready to leave.

Zia picked up the vase and held it close to her. She couldn't tell him they were from some stranger she met in Nebraska. Bryce would be angry and overprotective. She needed a lie and she needed one quickly.

"They're from the nurses," she lied through her teeth. "Yes, each nurse picked one flower to give to me. They were all very happy that the baby and I are going to be alright."

Bryce smiled and leaned over to kiss her cheek, "That's very sweet of them. Are you ready to go home?"

Zia wanted to say no but instead she nodded her head and smiled back at him.

The drive home seemed long and Zia hugged the vase of flowers the whole ride there. They were a symbol of how easy it was for her to lie, but they were also a symbol of safety in a place full of danger and mistrust. There was something inside of her, telling her to trust Willem. Something about him seemed safe. She was convinced that she would never see him again, but that was how she felt after the meeting in Nebraska, so she held on to hope.

When they got home, Bryce started unpacking the car while Zia waited at the door for him to open it. A minute hadn't even passed before his phone rang. He answered it, shouted at whoever was on the other side for a while, and then hung up.

"There's a problem at the office and I have to go," he confessed.

"That's okay," Zia insisted. "You go and do what you have to do, I'll just make something to eat and watch something until you get back."

"Only if you're sure," Bryce contested but he had already begun unlocking the door for Zia as if he had already decided to go. Zia nodded her head in response. "I'll be back as soon as I can," he leaned forward, avoiding the vase of flowers and her belly, and kissing her. "Don't go anywhere near the stairs until I come back. I don't want you climbing those stairs by yourself."

Zia certainly wasn't about to argue with that, "Okay, I'll stay downstairs."

She waved to Bryce as he jumped in the car and drove off with her bags still in the trunk. At least she didn't need anything in them just yet. She went inside and locked the door behind her. She turned the knob and pulled on it to make sure it was locked. No point in taking any chances. She gave the flowers some water and placed them in the middle of the counter in the kitchen. She stood and admired them for a moment. The house was silent and empty, but Zia remembered it wasn't entirely empty.

"Bugs?" She called out, "Bugs, where are you boy?"

Before she could finish speaking she heard his claws scraping against the tiled floor as he came rushing into the kitchen to greet her. He jumped up on her knees and began sniffing her all over. She smelled strange but he knew it was her. That was all Zia needed to make her feel better. She laughed at all the excited and silly noises Bugs made and her laughter only made him more excited.

Zia and Bugs lounged on the couch, eating snacks, and watching movies while they waited for Bryce to come home. Bugs eventually fell asleep. Zia couldn't bring herself to be so relaxed, even with Bugs there. She thought that she would never feel safe in this house again, and it seemed a shame not to feel safe in your own house.

The movie finished and she sat in silence for a while. The silence was dangerous and frightening. The tension built up until her phone vibrated and started ringing on the couch beside her. Zia screamed and jumped up off the couch. Bugs woke up barking, even though he had no idea what he was barking at. He ran around in circles barking at whatever might have made Zia scream but he stopped eventually when he realized there was nothing there. Zia sighed and breathed in heavily. She calmed herself down with a few breathing exercises and then answered the phone.

She didn't check who it was but she assumed it would be Bryce.

"Hello," she spoke into the speaker.

There was silence on the other end, but it wasn't complete silence. She could hear there was someone there. There was someone breathing ever so slightly into the speaker. She pulled the phone away from her face to look at the caller ID, but it said Unknown. She put the phone back to her ear.

"Hello! Who is this?" her voice took on a more serious and angry tone. "Who is this? Answer me now or I'm hanging up!"

"It's good to see you're back home and healthy again," the voice came through the speaker calmly and quickly before they hung up.

Zia's jaw dropped to the floor and her body went numb. The phone slipped out of her hand, bounced off of the couch, and hit the floor. The screen cracked and Bugs started barking. Zia was frozen in place. The voice sent bumps all over her body and made her head spin. The voice made her blood freeze and her skin crawl. There were so many thoughts in her head but there was only one thought that mattered above the rest. One thought stood out and screamed in her ears. One thought that made her want to run away and hide.

"He sounded like Baxter."

Chapter
SIX

A MONTH HAS PASSED SINCE THAT PHONE CALL AND Zia still refused to answer her phone. Bryce had to get her a new one after she dropped her last one. She kept it on silent. That way if it did ring she wouldn't be tempted to check who it is or answer it. She was sure she was losing her mind but that voice sounded like Baxter's voice and she wasn't about to relive that nightmare.

She started going back into the office. Bryce insisted she stay at home and work from there but she refused. She didn't let him know why but the truth was that she wasn't prepared to stay in that house by herself all day. If Bryce was going to the office, then so would she.

Zia found she was nervous all the time and the slightest thing annoyed and frightened her. Her anxiety came back and worse this time. Almost any stranger could set her off. She refused to go back on those pills that ruled her life less than a year ago. She started making things instead. She found keeping her hands busy helped keep her mind off of things.

Dazed and in a trance, she stared up at the hanging plaque she just finished crafting.

Inaction is a conscious decision.

The words spoke to her and she thought of nothing better to hang in her office. She could look up at it every day and know it is true. She learned that the hard way and she was determined not to make mistakes like that again.

She had a good office. It was far more luxurious than her first office in Fargo Tower and a lot more comfy and homely than the office they gave her in Sector 5. She had a modest amount of space, a great view with lots of light, and a lot of privacy. She loved it. Bryce had designed it of course, using everything he knew about her to make the perfect working space for her. She marveled at its simple yet perfect design. Bryce really knew her and loved her enough to show it in every way possible.

Her walls of serenity were shattered by the unnerving clinks of crashing, and banging noises. She pushed herself away from the desk and stepped out into the hallway. The long spiral staircase spread out in front of her and the hallway slowly filled with employees. They stepped out of their offices and leaned over the bannister to look downstairs but none of them were brave enough to venture down. The banging and crashing noises were added to the sound of screaming and the employees began to whisper and gossip amongst themselves.

Zia stepped forward, grabbed hold of the bannister with both hands, and she carefully leaned her head over. Jazmine screamed and yelled expletives downstairs while the office manager Carlos tried his best to calm her down. She waved her arms around angrily and Carlos had to duck and dodge as she swung at him.

"This is bullshit!" Jazmine yelled at him, growling and baring her teeth like an animal.

"Miss Fairfield, please. Please, you need to calm down," Carlos begged and pleaded in between his dodging.

Everyone seemed afraid of Jazz, but Zia was curious, and just a little annoyed. Jazz always took every opportunity she could to grab attention and she had a terrible habit of acting like a child. However, this was the first time Zia has seen her like this. She resembled a wild beast who'd just lost its dinner.

"All of you go back into your offices," Zia instructed the employees around her. She kept a calm and respectful tone and stature. "Everything is fine, now get back to work."

Zia headed down the stairs as the employees did as they were told. Zia held onto the bannister with both hands and took each step carefully. She climbed down slowly but kept her composure. She reached the lobby just as Jazmine grabbed hold of a vase and flung it across the room.

It shattered and the sound echoed through the building. Zia rolled her eyes. Jazz may be worth billions but that doesn't mean you can go around destroying $35,000 vases while throwing a temper-tantrum and acting like an unmannered toddler.

"God she is annoying," Zia thought to herself.

Zia decided to take control of the situation. Someone has to keep a level head in these situations, after all. She took a deep breath, held her head up and walked toward Jazz and Carlos.

"Carlos," she spoke clearly and calmly. There was an air of authority around her. "Go lock the front door, please. I don't want any clients walking in on this. When you're finished you can go take calls up in the conference room until further notice."

"Yes ma'am." Carlos ran to the front door and locked it as instructed. Then he headed for the stairs, making sure to keep far away from Jazz on his way.

"Oh," Zia remembered just as he started climbing the stairs. "Please call Mr. Fink and ask him to come back to the office as quickly as possible."

Carlos nodded and ran up the stairs, taking them two at a time.

Zia turned her attention to Jazmine.

"Now for the hard part," she thought.

She approached Jazmine from behind as she frantically searched for another object to destroy. Her breathing was harsh and ragged. She turned to face Zia. The crazed expression on her face startled Zia, but she remained calm. Jazmine's eyes are bulging out of her head, her lips are protruding, and she has her teeth bared. Her fried raven tresses are splayed across her face and she didn't seem to recognize her surroundings or Zia. She's a wild animal.

Zia, being in flats and only 5'2" at the moment, felt like a dwarf in a giant's shadow as Jazmines 5'7" stature towered over her.

"Jazmine, honey, it's Zia," she spoke quietly and calming while taking fractional steps toward her. She had her arms out in front of her and she reached for Jazmine's shoulders.

"Don't touch me!" Jazmine screeched.

Zia snatched her arms away and took a step back. "Okay, I won't touch you. What's wrong?"

"What?" Jazmine could barely breath and her face twisted into something that no longer resembled a human being. "What's wrong? What's wrong! Someone is contesting my piece of shit father's will. That's what's wrong!"

Jazmine grabbed the slightly ripped and crumbled documents off of Carlos' desk and waved them in the air as if to showcase them. Zia could only guess they were in that state because of Jazmine. Her head spun. How could someone be contesting Baxter's will? He had no living descendants or next of kin besides Jazmine as far as Zia knew. Who could possibly contest the will?

Zia wanted to take the documents and view them but Jazmine's behavior was too erratic and unpredictable. She couldn't risk her lashing out and hitting her stomach. Zia stood perfectly still, remained calm, and cradled Damien in her hands. All she could do was wait for Jazmine's shock and anger to dissipate.

Eventually Jazz grew tired and she began to teeter backwards. Zia rushed forward and grabbed her by the arms before she could fall over. She helped her to one of the clients chairs against the wall and she sat her down.

"It's okay honey, just relax," Zia spoke in a soothing voice, the way she would have back when Jazmine was still her friend. She'd been acting this whole time and there was no reason to stop now. "I'll get you some water."

Zia calmly walked over to the water dispenser and grabbed one of the plastic cups. She filled it up and walked back. As she lifted the cup to Jazz's lips she heard a key rattling in the front door. They both turned their attention to the door as Bryce unlocked it and walked in. His eyes darted from Zia to Jazz before he threw his briefcase to the floor and rushed over to them.

"What happened?" He held Zia's belly in both his hands while Zia explained the past events to him.

"She just went crazy. She mentioned something about her father's will being contested. I told the other employees to stay up stairs and continue working. I haven't seen the documents yet."

Bryce gazed into Zia's eyes for the longest time. He held her face by her chin and turned it from side to side, inspecting her for any damage.

"I'm fine," she reassured him. "We're fine," she added looking down at her belly.

He rubbed her stomach carefully and the love flowed through him into Zia and the baby. The concern in his eyes was intense. Then he turned to Jazmine, rested his hands against the arms of the chair, and leaned over her.

"Jazmine, tell me what's going on," his voice took on a more serious and professional tone.

Still dazed, she shoves the papers at him. She shot a wicked glance towards Zia's gargantuan wedding ring, and Zia caught it for a second before she quickly averted her eyes.

Bryce paced back and forth in a small semi-circle while skimming through the tattered documents in his hands. After reading each page he drops them on the chair beside Jazmine.

"Jazmine? Jazmine, look at me." Jazmine lazily lifted her head up to look at him. "Anyone can contest a will. Anyone at all. It doesn't mean that a judge will find merit. Most of the time, they don't."

Zia watched Jazmine's facial expression morph into something more human-like and less depressed. The light re-enters her eyes and she even manages a smile.

"So it might not be a next of kin?" she asked.

"Jazz, you were his only next of kin."

"He had a lot of secrets. For all I know, he has fathered a dozen children. What if?"

Bryce cut her off, "You can't drive yourself crazy with what if's. Find out who this—," he picked the documents up again, scanned the first page quickly, and then dropped them down. "Find out who this Willem Nickels is and then we can go from there."

Zia swallowed her tongue in order to stop herself from gasping. Her pulse quickened and the blood rushed to her ears. Her heartbeat pumped in her head and she felt like she was going to fall over. Thoughts rush through her head, each one of them trying to find a reason to leave the room.

"Let me go upstairs and get you a cool towel and a hair brush," Zia blurted out with the most genuine smile she could force, but she couldn't help giggling nervously. "I'll just check on the employees as well and then I'll be right back."

Bryce nodded and Zia made her way to the staircase.

"Zia!" Bryce shouted out, making her jump a little. She turned to face him. "What are you doing? Use the elevator. It's safer for you and the baby."

Zia caught herself and tried not to look guilty as she walked calmly to the elevator. She pressed the button to close the doors and as soon as they did the swearing began.

"Shit! Shit, shit, shit."

There was so much anger boiling inside her but it was mixed with fear and confusion. She trusted Lem. She trusted him like she had trusted people like Baxter and Bryce, and just like them he let her down. What kind of relative could he be? Maybe he isn't a relative. Bryce said anyone can contest a will, but why would Lem do that? These are all the thoughts that rushed through Zia's mind as the elevator took her up. She was confused and she needed answers. She deserved answers.

As soon as the elevator doors opened she rushed into her office, grabbed her phone out of her purse, and texted him. Her fingers type at the speed of light. She can barely breathe. She remembered why she was up there and quickly retrieved a hairbrush while waiting for a reply. She took the hairbrush and her phone to the bathroom just down the hall. She worked quickly at dampening a wash cloth with cold water when she heard a jingle from her phone she nearly threw the brush in her other hand.

Zia dropped everything and quickly checked her phone.

"I am not the next of kin, but I was appointed as the executor of the estate. If you'd like to know more, then meet me. I won't discuss this via text."

Zia rolled her eyes. Lem had been begging her to meet up with him ever since she left the hospital, but she always refused. She liked him.

She enjoyed talking with him and she would like nothing more than to meet with him somewhere. She couldn't risk Bryce finding out. She had also learned her lesson. The last time she met a charming stranger it was Baxter, and she would never forget how that turned out. This was a sneaky way of getting her to finally agree to a meet up.

She replied and agreed to meet with him. He had played his hand and won. He must have known that someone contesting the will would make her curious.

She checked in with the employees to make sure they were continuing with their usual duties and to inform them that everything is fine. She fetched Carlos and the both of them headed downstairs with brush and wash cloth in hand. The lobby is empty. Carlos returns to his desk as Zia begins her search for Bryce and Jazz.

She glanced outside but they weren't there, then she headed back up the stairs. She checked Jazz's office but it was empty. She approached Bryce's office and pulled on the handle. The door is locked. She knocked and waited.

"Bryce?" She called out when there was no answer.

"Why would the door be locked if he's here?" She thought while she waited. They all only lock their doors when they're leaving for the day. He's never locked the door while he is inside his office. She spots movement inside and she tries to peer through the frosted glass to see who it is. Bryce yanks the door open and Zia steps back shocked. She tries to scan the room behind him but he is keeping the door closed and only poking his head out.

"Why was the door locked?"

"I was on an important call and didn't want to be disturbed." Bryce replied but something about his answer didn't sit right with Zia.

"Isn't that why you ask Carlos to hold all your calls?"

"That wouldn't stop someone from walking through the door like you almost did. That would've distracted me."

It just didn't make sense to Zia and she only grew more suspicious of him. Zia found herself in no mood to argue with him and just left it at that.

"Where's Jazmine? I brought her a cool towel and hairbrush."

Bryce paused before answering, "Uh, she left."

Zia raised her eyebrows. Now she knows that something is wrong by the way he answered. He didn't seem sure of his own reply.

"Oh okay. Well, I'm going to leave early too. Do you think you can handle things?"

Bryce nodded, "Of course. Go home and get some rest. You're still flushed."

Zia was sure that she was, but not for the reasons that Bryce thought. Zia walked away and did her best not to think about how strange Bryce was acting. Why was he keeping the door closed like that? Why didn't he seem convinced by his own answers? What was he hiding from her?

ZIA DIDN'T GO HOME. SHE MESSAGED LEM AND SET UP A meeting with him. She drove to the café he chose, sat down at a table near the back, away from any windows, and she waited for him to arrive.

She was so stressed that every sound made her jump in her seat. Finally he walked through the door and headed towards her. He took the seat across from her and placed his briefcase on the table.

"Hello Zia," he smiled. "It's nice to see you again."

"We don't have time for pleasantries," Zia snapped. "Tell me who is contesting Baxter's will now so we can get this over and done with. You have no idea how much this is screwing my life up right now."

Lem looked taken back for a second, but then his face took on a more serious look. He opened up the briefcase and started shuffling through the documents he had inside it. He selected a few and took them out.

"Do you know how wills work?" he asked Zia. "Do you know that if a person wishes to, they can leave everything they own to almost anyone they want when they die, and they can rewrite their will whenever and however many times they want to." He explained and Zia just nodded to everything he was saying. She knows how wills work, everyone does. "Therefore, if Baxter, or should I say Dwight, choose to rewrite his will at the last moment, just before his death, as long as it was done legally then he could have willed everything to anyone he wanted to." Lem shuffled through the few pages in his hands, picked out one, and handed it to Zia. "He did change his will almost a week before his death. He willed everything he owned, money, estates, companies…, everything to one Zia Lennox."

Zia's eyes scanned the document. It was Baxter's will and right at the end of it she saw her name, just above Dwight's signature. She gasped and tears welled up in her eyes. She looked up at Lem whose eyes twinkled as a smile spread from one ear to the other.

"He willed it all to you Zia, and with this document you have the right to contest his daughter Jazmine for everything," he paused for effect, "and there is a very good chance that you will win in court."

"Why?" Was all Zia could manage to say for a while. "Why would he will it all to me?"

"There are many reasons why people change their wills at the last moment. It could be that he no longer trusted or loved anyone but you. He could not have wanted to leave his possessions in anyone else's hands. We'll never truly know why he willed everything to you, but what we do know is that you can contest his daughter."

"But she's his daughter! Bryce said that anyone can contest a will but the court won't always merit it. What makes you think I can contest his daughter?" Zia wasn't even sure why she was asking the question. Why would she want to contest it? She doesn't care about Baxter's will. She has enough money of her own and she doesn't need his.

"You have one thing on your side that will have any court ruling in your favor."

"What is that?"

"There are only two people right now who have the right to take possession of everything that Dwight Fairfield owned, you and his daughter. However, only one of you is responsible for his death."

Zia's head was spinning. She didn't know what to do, she didn't know what she wanted to do. She told Lem she had to go. She needed to get out of there and away from him. She had the feeling that the only reason he was getting close to her was because of the will. Her heart shattered when she thought that it was all a setup. Willem wasn't interested in being her friend, he was just doing his job as executor of the estate.

Zia was driving home until she realized that she had left her laptop at the office and she needed to get something off of it for work. She was so caught up in Baxter again that she had forgotten it. If she left it to the morning she knew that Bryce would get upset with her because they were documents from an important client.

She glanced at her watch, the office would be closed now but she had a key, and Bryce works late sometimes. She would be in and out, and she might be able to talk to Bryce about a few things.

The office felt eerie after closing time. She wasn't wearing heels but her every step echoed through the building as if she were. It was getting dark as the sun started to set. She made her way up the stairs slowly. She glanced around. Every shadow was hiding a monster that she didn't want to be left alone with. Maybe she was paranoid, but right now she had every right to be.

She checked Bryce's office first but the door was locked and she couldn't see or hear anyone inside. She went to her office and packed up her laptop. She could just print out the documents but that would take longer and she wanted to get out of there quickly.

She locked her office and started towards the stairs, but something told her it wasn't a good idea. Something made her turn around and go to the elevator instead. She pressed the button to call the elevator when her phone jingled in her purse. She picked it up and read the text. It was from Lem.

"Zia, where are you? I think you may be in danger. I got a call from an unknown number asking me about the will. I didn't tell them anything but they wanted me to confirm that your name was on the will. Zia, they know that Dwight willed everything to you, and they didn't sound happy."

As Zia read the text her hand started to shake and every bone in her body froze in place. Who could it have been that called Lem. Was it her stalker that has been sending her all of those emails? Was she in danger? Did they know where she was? She didn't know what to do. She was alone and she was too scared to move.

The elevator dinged as it arrived on her floor. Suddenly she regained her strength to move and she stepped into the elevator. She needed to get out of here. She needed to get home where Bryce could protect her. She reached for the button to close the doors but as her finger pressed down on it the power cut out. The light in the elevator went off and it was frozen in place. None of the buttons worked. Zia cursed her luck as a sound echoed through the building.

Zia gasped and stepped back further into the elevator. She couldn't be sure but it sounded like footsteps running by the stairs. It echoed through the whole building, so the sound could have come from any-where. One thing was for sure, she wasn't alone. Zia breathed in deeply and stepped out of the elevator. Someone had cut off the power and was running around the building somewhere. She needed to get out of here and her only option now was to go down the stairs as quickly as she could.

Each step she took towards the stairs echoed and she felt like she would never reach them. She walked as quietly as she could but her steps still echoed through the building. She reached the top of the staircase and grabbed hold of the bannister. She glanced down to the lobby below but there was no one there. She let out a soft sigh and took the first step. That was when she heard them. In a split second she heard the footsteps running up behind her, she gasped, let go of the bannister and tried to turn around towards the direction of the footsteps. She felt a weight against the side of her shoulder and the weight pushed her backwards.

Her life flashed before her eyes as the world around her blurred. She continued to turn around. Maybe she could see the face of her attacker before the end. She turned, but all she saw was darkness as she fell. She tumbled all the way to the bottom of the spiral staircase but she lost her sight and fell unconscious about half way down. She was left to lie at the bottom of the staircase, blood pouring from a small cut in her head and from her broken nose. Her one leg was twisted in an unnatural posses-sion and if she were awake she would be screaming from the pain.

Chapter
SEVEN

THE HOSPITAL WAS A COLD HOME, BUT SHE HAD TO LIVE there for almost a month. They kept telling her that she would be able to go home faster if she cooperated and took her treatments. Zia didn't want to go home. She fought them and refused every treatment they wanted to give her. Why would she want to go home when she felt safer here than she did there?

Zia's heart shattered the moment she woke up and looked down at her belly. It was sticking out but not as much as she was used to. When she tried to move there was sharp pain all over her body, but the pain was worse by her stomach. She didn't want to admit it, but she knew what it meant. Later, Bryce came to visit her and confirmed her belief. She had lost the baby. The news was more than Zia could handle but Bryce had more news for her to swallow.

Bryce confirmed for Zia that his inheritance was based on the consummation of their marriage and their ability to produce an heir to Weingart. Zia already knew that after reading that document her stalker emailed to her. It was different hearing it from him. It was as if their marriage and her baby were all just things to him. Things that would help him get his inheritance. She was sure that she meant more to him than that, but right now she felt as if she meant nothing.

To make matters worse, Bryce informed Zia that Bugs was missing. He had disappeared the night she fell down the stairs. Bryce said he ran away. Something told Zia not to believe that. Bugs was a good boy and she knew he wouldn't just run away for no reason. For now there was nothing she could do about it. Bryce was doing everything possible to find him and Zia needed time to recover. She would be out there on the streets looking for Bugs herself if she could, because right now, he was all she had left.

SHE WOKE UP SCREAMING. IT WAS THE EIGHTH TIME SINCE getting home from the hospital that she had woken up like this. She had nightmares on and off before the accident. Now they just keep getting worse to the point where she woke up screaming for help. Bryce stopped running to her aid a long time ago. Now he let Sally do it. Bryce hired Sally after she got out of the hospital to live with them and help Zia with her recovery.

Right on cue Sally ran into the room with a wet towel and a glass of water. She placed the glass of water down and used the towel to wipe the sweat off Zia's face. Then she gave her the glass of water to drink.

"It's alright now, it was just a bad dream," Sally consoled her. "You're awake now, so no need to worry about it anymore."

Zia drank the water and looked at the empty part of the bed beside her. "Where's Bryce?"

"Oh! Umm, he had a late night at work again and fell asleep on the couch downstairs. Do you want me to go get him?"

Zia thought for a moment and put the glass down, "No." She finally replied. "I don't need his help anymore."

Sally seemed confused and a bit uncomfortable. She wasn't sure what to do or say in this situation.

"Has anyone called about Bugs yet?"

"No one's called unfortunately," Sally picked up the glass and the towel. "Would you like anything else?"

"Turn on my PC on your way downstairs. I'm going to do some work to make myself tired again."

Sally nodded and left the room quickly. Zia couldn't get back to sleep, not knowing that there were just more nightmares about Baxter waiting

for her.

During her sleepless night Zia found an old, crumpled up piece of paper in one of her purses. It was the name and number for a hypnotist her therapist had given to her. With her nightmares getting worse, she decided now was the best time to give hypnotism a try. She knew the dreams were trying to tell her something, but for some reason she is blocking it out of her memories.

"Remember Sally, don't tell Bryce where I'm going. Just tell him I insisted on getting some fresh air and alone time." Zia instructed.

Sally was uncomfortable but she nodded her head. Bryce might be the one that hired her but her job was to take care of Zia. This was part of the job now. Zia left the house before Bryce had the chance to wake up and drove to the hypnotist's house. Zia knew a lot of therapists and other kinds of medical professionals that worked out of their home, but she had never seen a house so tranquil and open like this one.

It seemed like his whole house was designed like a greenhouse in the Amazon rainforest. Everywhere she looked there was a different plant thriving in its environment. It was beautiful and welcoming. She thought that one day she wanted to design a home like this one.

"Please have a seat," he said after walking her through the house into the seating area. "You said your name was Zia?"

"Yes, Zia Fink, and you're Dr. Herb Gardener?"

He giggled and nodded his head, "Yes but you can just call me Herb, although herbs are about the only things I don't grow here." He laughed out loud startling Zia. Even though Zia noticed the joke she was too stressed to laugh. "My parents thought themselves very funny, you see. They named me Herb and told me they wanted me to be a Herb Gardener. I am a gardener but I guess I didn't live up to their dreams exactly. Anyways, that's enough about me. Let's talk about your problems shall we. Why have you decided to see a hypnotist?"

"My therapist actually gave me your details. I've been having nightmares lately, horrible ones, but there's something about them that makes me think they're more than dreams. They seem familiar, almost like memories. That's what I told her and she referred me to you."

Herb nodded his head as he listened intently to Zia.

"Have you experienced some sort of trauma in the past?"

Zia tried not to laugh at the question. Lately it seemed like her whole life was a trauma. She nodded her head in response.

"People who experience trauma often block the memories of that trauma. They lock them away deep inside their mind. However, the mind is a tricky thing and it cannot be fooled forever. Eventually the memories will start slipping through that wall we've built in front of them. They often do this through dreams." He adjusted in his seat by leaning back and lifting one leg over the other. "This wall I'm talking about is known as a mind block. I can help you break through this wall and access these blocked off memories through hypnotism. I must warn you it is not an easy process and, depending on how far back these memories go, it will have to be done over multiple sessions. Are you ready for that?"

Zia was silent for a moment while she thought about it. If she did this the nightmares could go away, or they could get worse. Perhaps she blocked these memories for a reason. Maybe it was better that she forget them. It was difficult to forget something that plagued you every time you closed your eyes. She needed to know the truth. It was important for some reason that much she knew, otherwise she wouldn't keep reliving the memories every time she went to sleep.

"I'm ready."

Herb smiled for a second and then his face went hard and professional. "Lie down on the couch please."

Zia turned to her side and spread her legs out on the couch. She adjusted her clothes and moved around a bit until she was comfortably on her back. She expected Herb to come closer but he remained in his seat.

"Close your eyes," he instructed and Zia did as she was told. "We can assume that these memories are connected to the trauma you suffered, so what I want you to do is think of a time before the trauma. Think of a time when you were perfectly happy and content with your life."

Zia ran through her memories, looking for a time she was happy before it all happened. She can remember being happy after Baxter died. She had married Bryce, they had completed the merger of the two companies and she was sporting a baby bump. That moment was perfect. She had the perfect husband, the perfect best friend, and the perfect life. She held that happy moment for only a second before those pictures she received from Kevin shattered her world.

She needed to think further back, to a time before Baxter, a time where the world made sense and she was happy with it for the most part. She found it. That one small spot in her life where things seemed good. She had just met Bryce and had read the first few pages of Chiseled Bone. She hadn't met Baxter yet and the only reason he was in her life was because his book was going to carry her to the top. Jazz was still her best friend and life seemed good.

"Have you found it?" Zia nodded and Herb's voice took on a softer, kinder tone. "Good, now I want you to sit in that moment for a while. Nothing else exists except for that moment." Zia had never been hypnotized before but this was nothing like what she'd seen in movies. This was different in some way. "Now I know you don't want to relive the trauma, but that's what we're going to do. We're going to go through each memory slowly, and with each memory resurfacing you may find new memories being pulled up with the rest. Are you ready to proceed?"

Zia wanted to stay in that moment of pure happiness for a while longer, but she wasn't here to relive the good old days. She was here for answers.

"Yes, I'm ready."

"SALLY!" ZIA CALLED out from upstairs, while Sally was in the kitchen making them lunch. "Sally I need your help with this!" Sally came running up the stairs and into the nursery to see Zia holding one side of the crib.

"I thought Mr. Fink was going to do that when he got back from work."

"Mr. Fink said he would move it last week as well but he didn't. I want to get this over and done with, okay? Now help me move it downstairs before the van gets here."

Zia had told Bryce she wanted to redo the nursery around the same time she started going to see Dr. Herb. She couldn't do any work with it right next to her. It was a constant reminder of the fact that someone took Damien away from her. She never told anyone about her suspicions but she knows that she didn't just fall down the stairs that night. Someone was in the building with her. Someone turned the power off so she couldn't use the elevator. She felt someone push her, even if she didn't see them, she knows that someone tried to kill her that night, but instead they killed her baby.

Sally rushed over and grabbed the other side of the crib. They struggled to move it but eventually they got it out of the room and down the stairs. They put it by the front door so it would be easy to move out of the house and into the van. Zia decided to put everything that would remind her of Damien into storage. She didn't have any plans for the room yet. She would rather it stand empty than stand as a reminder of what she lost that night.

Zia and Sally leaned against the crib huffing and puffing. Sally had broken more of a sweat than Zia, but the sweat was probably from stress and not from carrying the crib.

"I'll get us something to drink," Sally said as she rushed to the kitchen.

Zia ran after her and hopped up on the barstool by the overhanging counter. She had felt a lot more energetic lately. She hated that it was probably because the baby was gone. She also felt better because of her trips to Dr. Herb. She hadn't learned anything yet, and that's what she expected would happen. Herb did say it would be a slow process. She'd been to him for three sessions and still no answers, but she also hasn't had a nightmare since, so she sees that as progress.

Sally poured them both a glass of lemonade but before Zia could take a sip of hers there was a knock at the door. Zia sighed loudly, making Sally laugh.

"Maybe it's the van?" Sally suggested.

"If it is then they're an hour early," Zia got up and headed towards the door.

It's been ages since she answered the door without looking through the peephole but today she wasn't thinking about safety. Sally was here and she felt safe enough. She opened the door but there was nobody standing on the other side. Her brows furrowed as she stepped out onto the porch. She looked around but her foot hit something as she stepped out.

She looked down and saw a box on the porch in front of her. The moment she set eyes on it, a horrible smell hit her in the face. Tears burnt her eyes and she quickly brought her hand up to cover her mouth and nose. There was a low rumbling sound coming from inside the box and the bottom of it seemed soggy, as if some kind of liquid was trying to seep out. There was a note on top of the box written in black ink with rough and childish handwriting.

Zia used her other hand to wipe the tear from her eyes so she could see the note. She bent down closer to read it as Sally appeared at the door behind her.

"What the hell is that god awful smell?" Sally muttered through her covered mouth and blocked nose.

"He protected you so well. Too bad you never taught him how to shut up!"

Zia gasped.

"It can't be," Zia stuttered with tears in her eyes. "Please don't let it be him."

Zia swiped the note out of the way and pulled the tape away from the box. She held her breath and tried to ignore the smell as she opened the box. The tears she was holding back burned in the back of her throat and made her choke. She didn't know if she should open it slowly or fast. She threw the sides open and Sally let out a scream behind her. Zia wanted to scream but she couldn't find her voice. She was frozen in front of the box as the flies swarmed out of it and hit her in the face.

She could see now that the liquid seeping through the bottom was blood and the rumbling sound was the flies trapped in the box with the body. It looked like someone had ripped the body apart limb by limb. Zia would never have recognized him if it weren't for Bugs' collar sitting at the bottom covered in blood.

Sally ran back into the house screaming the whole way. Zia wanted to move. She wanted to scream, cry, break down, or curse at the sky. She couldn't do any of that. She was frozen and she couldn't move. She didn't want to believe this was happening. The one constant good thing in her life was lying dead in front of her and she couldn't even recognize him through all the blood.

Zia heard Sally speak behind her and snapped her out of it.

"Hello, is this the police?"

Zia panicked. She grabbed the note from the ground and stuffed it into her pocket. Calling the police is a good idea. A dead body has just been dumped on her doorstep, but for some reason she didn't want them seeing the note. She didn't want them knowing more than they should. If the hypnotism doesn't work then that stalker is her only other access to the truth. Yes, she was sure it was him that kidnapped and slaughtered her beloved Bugs. She hated him. She wanted to kill him and cut him into pieces like he had done to her dog. If the police got to him then she wouldn't be able to do any of that.

Another thought entered her head. Perhaps it wasn't the stalker, after all what reason would he have to kill Bugs if all he did was send her emails. With this thought in her mind she blamed Jazmine. She didn't want to believe that Jazmine was capable of something like that, but Zia remembered how easy it was for her to shoot her father in the head. To some people, killing a dog would be easier than killing a human being. Bugs didn't like Jazmine. Bugs growled and barked at Jazmine all the time. It is possible that Jazmine got fed up with that and took care of it. It would also tie in with the fact that Zia is certain Jazmine pushed her down the stairs the first time. It was all fitting together in her head like a big puzzle.

While Sally was on the phone to the police, Zia needed to make a call as well. She wanted someone there but she wasn't sure who. She brought up Bryce's number on her phone. He was at work but he would rush over the moment he heard that she needed him, but the problem was that she didn't need him. She decided to send him a text instead. If she didn't say anything he would wonder why and she couldn't tell him how she didn't trust him or feel safe with him anymore.

The reality of the situation hit her as the police filed into her house to ask questions. First there were only the two of them. Then more showed up to take photos of the box and remove it as evidence. Zia collapsed onto the couch. She couldn't speak, she couldn't think, she was seconds away from bursting into tears. There was so much going on that it only dawned on her now that her best friend was dead. Her sweet boy had been slaughtered and delivered to her in pieces. She wanted to be sad, she needed to be sad. There was no time for her to mourn Bugs now, there was only time for revenge.

She was determined now more than ever to get some questions answered and find out who this stalker is, and bring Jazmine down to her knees.

NINE

"ARE YOU AT that comfortable, happy place?" Dr. Herb asked while holding his pen and notebook at the ready.

Zia moved slightly on the couch while keeping her eyes shut and imagining she was sitting at her desk in the Fargo Tower. She had just discovered Chiseled Bone and her life was at a perfect and happy point. This was her comfortable and happy place.

"Yes, I am," she replied.

"Good, remember that you can return to this place whenever you want to. It is hidden behind a door in your mind and all you have to do is open that door," he jotted down a note. "When you're ready, you can open the door and step out into your mind."

Zia, knowing that she is lying comfortably on Dr. Herbs couch, imagined herself standing up from her desk. She walked towards the door to her office and opened it up. Outside wasn't Forgo Tower but a long empty hall with doors as far as she could see. This was her mind. Dr. Herb had helped her create it this way. Each door led to a part of her mind or a memory. All she had to do was find the right door and open it up, and so far they hadn't had much luck finding the door she needed. She hadn't found any answers yet.

She walked down the hallway filled with doors and wondered which one she would open this time. The doors were all the same bright white and they weren't labeled. They all looked exactly the same. She had no idea which memory she would find behind each door. All she knew was that the further she went down the hall, the older the memories would be. There was no method to it. She just chose a door and opened it, hoping there is something useful behind it.

That's what she did now. She opened one of the doors and walked in, and just like pressing play on a movie, her memory started playing in her head. It didn't take long for her to recognize the scene. Baxter was sitting beside her and across the table from them were Amahle and Kungawao. She never really forgot this night, but she let it slip to the back of her mind. Amahle was spinning her story about Zia being a descendant of some kind of African royalty.

Zia gasped.

"What is it?" Dr. Herb asked, sitting up in his seat. "Have you found an important memory? Remember if it is too much for you all you have to do is close the door and return to your happy place."

Zia heard his words, but they were miles away. She couldn't believe that she would let such an important memory like this one slip to the back of her mind. She forced herself to look at the memory of Baxter's face in this moment. He is so convinced and intrigued by Amahle's story. He believes every word that she is saying. Zia thought to herself how trusting he became of her after that. She was able to sneak out of his arms and copy those files from his laptop that night. She would never have been able to do that if Baxter hadn't believed everything Amahle had said.

"That's it!" Zia cried out.

She closed the door and returned to her office before she could open her eyes, just like Dr. Herb had taught her. She sat up on the couch to see his very confused face.

"Have you found something?" He asked, with his notebook and pen at the ready.

Zia nodded with a triumphant smile spreading across her face, "Yes, I think I have."

Finding Amahle and Kungawao was a challenge. Zia hired Kevin again, something she thought she would never do after Baxter. He was the only one she could trust with this. She had their first names, had described how they look, and told him to look somewhere in Africa. Then she waited. Kevin went silent for almost a month then he sent her an email with their full names and their current address. Zia wasted no time going to see them.

She stood in front of their house and her heart was pounding in her head. This was the only way to get answers. This was her best chance at tearing Jazmine back down where she belonged. She raised her hand and knocked. Amahle opened the door and the moment she set her eyes on Zia they were filled with confusion, fear, and guilt.

"Zia!" she exclaimed, putting on her acting voice again. "What a surprise! It's good to see you again my queen."

"Cut the crap," Zia wasn't dealing with her bullshit again. She was far too much of a shy and quiet person to speak up back when they first met. Now she is stronger, and she's learned to speak her mind. "I've jumped through a lot of hoops to track you down and I'm not leaving here until you give me some answers."

The smile faded from Amahle's face and she glanced back into her house. She quickly stepped out with Zia and closed the door behind her.

"Okay, whatever you want, just get on with it," she whispered. "You need to get out of here before my husband sees you."

Zia smiled, for once things were going her way.

"We both know that story you spun to me and Baxter all those years ago was a load of shit," Zia said. "I need you to tell me who put you up to it. It was a girl named Jazmine wasn't it."

Amahle hesitated. She glanced around as if she was looking for a way to escape from Zia.

"I already have pictures of you and Jazmine together!" Zia raised her voice, hoping the threat of Amahle's husband hearing them would scare her into talking. "I have all the evidence I need to confirm that Jazmine put you up to telling that story. All I need now is for you to confirm it."

"Okay, okay, just keep it down," Amahle hissed at her. "You're right, a woman named Jazmine approached me and paid me to do that. She said that Baxter guy was very superstitious and she was playing a prank on him or something. She wanted me to tell that story and make it as convincing as possible. She paid me a lot and all I had to do was tell a story. I didn't think it was that big a deal. Please my husband, Kunga-wao, knew nothing about it. If he found out that I did that he'd be angry. You have to go now."

"Thank you," Zia muttered before she left.

That was it. That's all she needed and now she had more than enough reason to bring Jazmine down to her knees. She had the photos but that wasn't evidence enough. She needed to know for sure and now she did. Jazmine knew how her father would react to a story like that, so she set both him and her up. All of this confirmed Zia's suspicions that Jazmine made a plan to tear her father down and that she was using Zia as bait to lure him out and kill him.

Chapter
TEN

Life seems to have returned to normal for everyone, except for Zia. She was too busy planning her revenge to have a normal life. She'd lost everything and she would make sure that Jazmine would pay for it. The only way she could get back at Jazmine was to take away everything she has, just like she had done to her. The only thing Jazmine has is wealth and power. Those things won't be easy to take away, but Zia was clever and willing to do anything she needed to. She will get her revenge.

Zia walked down the stairs quietly and went into the living room to check on Bryce. He was still fast asleep on the couch. She'd been pulling away from him. She didn't want to fight with him and she knew that he loved her more than anything, but she also knew that he lied to her for a long time and that he was probably plotting with Jazmine from the beginning. Zia spent a long time feeling guilty about cheating on Bryce with Baxter. Bryce made her feel even guiltier when he found out and was angry at her. He had no right to act that way when he was doing the exact same thing behind her back and for longer than her as well.

Zia still hasn't figured out the significance of that video her stalker had sent her. How could Bryce and Jazmine have been together even before Zia met him? She thought about it as she headed to the kitchen to make some breakfast. Making breakfast just wasn't the same without Bugs jumping up her legs and begging for a treat. But she couldn't think about that now. There were plans that needed to be made. Bugs would get his revenge as well.

Zia had only just turned on the kettle and was fetching the milk from the fridge when she heard something slide in through the letter box at the front door. She was hesitant at first and glanced at the front door from behind the fridge door. She could see a single rigid white envelope. After having a dead and dismembered dog delivered to your front door how bad can one envelope be? Zia swallowed the lump in her throat and fetched it.

The envelope was addressed to Zia Lennox. Not Fink. "Oh no, not again," Zia thought. The last time she received a letter addressed to her maiden name it was from Kevin and it shattered her perfect world. There was no return address though and it didn't say who sent it. Zia carefully tore it open, fully expecting there to be fingers or something inside of it. She removed the documents from inside and read the note attached to the top of them.

> *"Even in death, I will always love you. If you received this, then I am long gone, and you should choose Bryce, but do not trust Jazmine. – Baxter."*

Zia read the note over and over again, but it still didn't make sense to him. Did Baxter know he was going to die? Did he know that Jazmine would be the one to kill him? Did he write this note anticipating his own demise? She wasn't going to get any more clues from the note, so she put it aside and read the accompanying documents.

She unfolded the document and found a holographic blue cashier's check for $746,228,132.18 and it was dated a week before Baxter's death. She turned her attention to the document. It was Baxter's will. This one was different from the one that Willem had shown her the night she got thrown down the stairs. That one just stated that everything Baxter owned should be given to her. This one included that, but it also has instructions for Zia to follow. Zia read the instructions and her face lit up. She found it! She found a way to get her revenge on Jazmine by taking away everything she has and tearing her to the ground.

Bryce walked in on Zia while she was reading the documents. She was so hypnotized by the plan forming in her head that she didn't even notice him.

"What is that?" he asked, snapping her out of her trance.

She looked up and she couldn't think of a lie to tell him, so she told him the truth.

"It's a letter from Baxter."

"ZIA, I WANT YOU TO THINK ABOUT THIS, LONG AND HARD, think about what you will be doing here," Willem instructed her. "Think about the consequences, not just for you but for everyone involved. Think about what this will do to your friendship with Jazmine."

Zia looked at him with a blank expression, "There is no friendship between me and Jazmine."

"What about your marriage with Bryce? This will affect that as well."

"I'll cross that bridge when I get to it," Zia sounded harsh but she maintained a professional attitude. "I want to do this."

"Okay," Willem sighed and looked over the will Baxter had sent to Zia once again. "It will be difficult but with me as your legal counsel and lawyer, we might just stand a chance at winning this thing."

"Good, because I want to take everything from her, I don't want to settle for less. I want everything that Baxter has willed to me."

Zia thought about it over and over again. She would have preferred Bryce to help her and be her lawyer but she knew that he would never agree to this. She planned to reveal that she is the rightful heir to Paradigm and then take everything from Jazmine. Bryce would never help her with that. Willem was more than capable and happy to help. This was going to be a difficult battle, but Zia was ready to go through it.

The war started with Willem sending a summons to Jazmine informing her that a new will had surfaced naming Zia the heir to Paradigm. Zia wasn't there to see it but she was sure Jazmine probably threw a few vases and maybe even a chair at the wall when she heard. Then the legal battle started. The first day Zia entered the court she was horrified to see that Bryce was acting as Jazmine's lawyer. Zia was filled with hatred.

She felt like she'd been stabbed in the back a hundred times in a row. She couldn't worry about that now. She had a war to win.

It was strange, watching Willem and Bryce fight in the court. They weren't actually fighting but each time one of them spoke, it felt like they were verbally attacking the other. Zia imagined it was all in her head. They were both just doing their jobs and trying to win the legal battle. Zia wasn't entirely sure what was going on most of the time, but Willem would catch her up on how well they were doing every time he sat down beside her and Bryce stood up to speak. So far they were doing well.

The legal battle lasted for months on end and each day that passed Bryce and Zia grew further apart. Eventually Zia didn't feel welcome in her own home and she did the only thing she could think of. She moved in with her parents. They of course welcomed her with open arms, but Zia assured them that she wouldn't bother them for too long. When she won this battle she'd be able to buy them all a mansion.

Finally the battle was nearing its end and Zia would learn the results. She had a knot growing in her stomach the whole day as she waited for the judge to return with his decision. The knot grew and grew until it felt like her whole body would crumple up and be consumed by it. Willem assured her that they were doing well and he had hope they would win. Zia didn't want to assume anything. If they lost this, then she'd thrown away everything she had for nothing.

"Hey Zee," Zia looked up and was shocked to see Jazmine standing in front of her. She had a sad but forced smile on her face. "Can we talk for a second?"

Zia glanced at Willem as if she was asking him for permission and he gave her a slight nod.

"Talk quickly and watch what you say," he instructed her as Zia stood up and walked after Jazmine.

"What do you want to talk about?" Zia spoke with an emotionless tone.

"I just want to know why. Why are you doing this? What did I do wrong?" Jazmine looked like she was ready to burst into tears, but Zia had seen her act before. She knew this was nothing more than an act.

"You can cut the act Jazmine, I know everything. I know about you and Bryce sneaking off for little dates. I have pictures of the two of you in bed, making out, holding hands, and I even have a video of the two of you together before Bryce even started working at Fargo Tower. That's just the start," Zia laid it all out on her. You can't teach someone a lesson if they don't know what they've done wrong. She decided not to tell her about anything else, the only thing she needed to know was that she betrayed her.

"Seriously?" Jazmine dropped her acting face and replaced it with anger. "That's why you're doing all this? You're ruining my life because I fucked your husband while you were out riding my father's dick? Wow, that's really mature of you Zia."

"It's a lot more complicated than that but I'm not going to bore your small mind with the details."

"What about Bryce, huh? What are you doing to him? He's the one that cheated on you, after all."

"I've forgiven Bryce for what he's done because he did the same thing that I did, but you Jazmine, you had no right to do what you did. You were supposed to be my friend and you betrayed me. Stabbed me in the back! You don't deserve forgiveness, you deserve ruin. Bryce is my husband now and I'm willing to work this out to the end if I need to."

"You can keep telling yourself that you forgive Bryce's trespasses and not mine because you're married, but that's not the reason."

"Whatever Jazz." Zia turned to walk away.

"It's desire."

"What?"

"It's because you desire him. It wouldn't matter if you were married or not, whether it was Bryce or a different man. You're willing to forgive his shit because you desire him. You desire a man, so you're anxious to forgive a man. You've yet to learn that your female friends and family are as important as any dick you'll ride this lifetime."

"Oh, that's fancy."

"You're a misogynist, Zee."

"I don't hate women Jazmine. I hate you!"

Zia turned away from Jazmine and walked back to Willem. She glanced over at Bryce who was watching their conversation. She hoped he didn't hear any of it. Before Zia could sit down they were called back into the courtroom.

"What's happening?" Zia asked Willem as they all filed back into the courtroom.

"The judge has made a decision."

THE JUDGE BROUGHT HIS GAVEL DOWN AND ZIA'S HEART jumped up into her throat. She won. Everything Baxter owned was hers. Everything except for a few small holdings like Spark, but Jazmine had already sold Spark, so Zia's plan worked. Jazmine was ruined and she had nothing left. Zia could continue with the rest of her plan. Her first act as majority shareholder and CEO of Paradigm was to dissolve the standing merger between Weingart and Paradigm. The two conglomerates will be separated once again and then Zia can move forward with getting rid of everything that would ever remind her of Baxter.

The separation wasn't easy, as board members of both companies challenged her in court. Willem stood by her side for it all and he said he'd do what he could, but the fight was not going in their direction. Zia had no real reason to separate the company, and Willem told her that if she couldn't find a reason, they would lose.

Zia was laying on her childhood bed thinking of a reason why the two companies need to be separated. A reason besides the fact that she wanted to tear Paradigm down to the ground. She could hear her mother cooking dinner in the kitchen and her father yelling at the television as if the people could hear him. There were boxes all over the place with her stuff in them.

"You really need to sort through all this stuff at some point," Zia's mother told her as she walked into the room.

Zia sat up quickly, "I didn't hear you coming up the stairs. There's no point in me sorting out the boxes, I won't be staying here for too much longer."

"That may be true, but a messy room equals a messy mind. You may be coming in here to think but you'll never think of anything in this clutter."

Zia looked around at the clutter and mess. It did make her feel uncomfortable and it crowded her head.

"Wise as ever mother," Zia smiled. "I'll sort through a few before dinner time."

Zia's mother left the room to finish her cooking while Zia hunkered down and started sorting through the boxes. She'd been looking through them for a good while when she came across one that looked older than the others. It seemed like it was filled with work items. A mouse pad, a few pens, and an old mug. Zia gasped upon realizing it was the box she packed the night Baxter attacked her in Fargo Tower.

She picked up the mug and a small, black object fell out of it and back into the box. Zia quickly reached into the box and grabbed it. It was a flash drive. She remembered! It must be the same flash drive she used to copy folders off of Baxter's laptop as evidence for Detective John.

Her curiosity got the better of her and she plugged it into her laptop. The last thing she wanted to do was relive those days with Baxter, but she couldn't remember what files she had copied over. Some part of her was dying to find out. She shuffled through the folders but the majority of them contained some kind of financial documents, all of them stamped Paradigm on the bottom. Zia wasn't very good when it came to the financials of a company, but even to her something didn't seem right about the numbers.

She emailed a few of the documents to Willem, hoping that he would be able to make heads or tails of them. Then she went to eat dinner with her parents.

Before Zia went to bed that night, she checked her emails and saw that Willem had replied.

"Where did you find these?"

She quickly typed out a response; *"They were on an old flash drive. I had copied some files from Baxter's laptop hoping they would incrimi-*

nate him. Why?"

She received an immediate reply; "These are incriminating alright. These documents are enough to prove Paradigm was involved in fraud. Zia, you just found the perfect card for us to play. We're going to win this battle tomorrow and separate Weingart and Paradigm for good."

ZIA STOOD UP IN COURT AS THE JUDGE LOWERED THE gavel down for the second time, once again ruling in her favor. Willem was right. The evidence on the flash drive wasn't just enough to stop the merger from finalizing but it was also enough to have an injunction filed against Paradigm.

Zia couldn't believe this was all happening. Her roughly put together plan is actually working out. She had torn Jazmine down to the ground, bankrupted her, and humiliated her. Now she can proceed with tearing down the last reminder of Baxter and watching it burn to ash. Paradigm would not survive her; she would make sure of that.

Everyone filed out of the court, Zia waited till everyone was gone before she left. She'd rather wait till the building was empty than get caught in the crowd. She did the same thing whenever she went to the cinema. She got up and headed towards the exit only to see Bryce waiting at the door for her. The expression on his face was strange. It looked as if he had been crying and she had never seen him that vulnerable before.

"Bryce," Zia whispered. "What are you doing here? I thought you didn't want to be involved in this anymore."

"That's not why I'm here," his voice was weak and harsh. "I don't care about the stupid merger, I don't care about these companies, I don't care about any of it. Come home Zia. That's all I care about. I want you to come home and I want us to get back to our lives."

Zia took a careful step towards him. She wished she could run to him and jump into his arms but she was afraid. She was afraid that he would let her fall. Zia had fallen so many times that she might break if she were to hit the floor again.

"You don't care why I've done all of this?" She asked. "You don't want to know why I've decided to take everything away from Jazmine? You don't care about the reasons I wanted to take Paradigm away from her?"

Bryce sighed, "I know you found out about me and Jazmine, and I know you probably hate me for it. I tore you down and made you hate yourself for cheating on me with Baxter and in the meantime I was doing the same thing with Jazmine. I understand that." Bryce stepped into the room and walked towards her, since she was taking her time to walk to him. "Even if you hate me and never want to see me again I needed to let you know how much I love you. Zia, I love you more than anything. What happened with Jazmine was pure pleasure. There was no love involved. I still kick myself every day when I think about what I did." Tears welled up in his eyes. "I would never forgive myself if I allowed the best thing that ever happened to me to walk out of my life without fighting for her. Zia, please come home and work this out with me." He dropped down to his knees, wrapped his arms around her waist, and buried his face in her stomach. "Please forgive me."

Zia stroked his head gently, running her nails through his hair. She looked down at him and a smile spread across her face. This was her first genuine smile in a long time.

"Bryce, my love, I forgave you the moment I found out the truth," she whispered in a soft, silky tone. "Go on then, take me home."

The ride home was quiet and calm, but blissful. Zia leaned her head against the window and watched the trees along the side of the road blur past. She hadn't driven down this road in a few months now, it seemed so new to her, but still familiar. Her mother was happy to hear she was on her way back home. Zia wasn't ready to admit it yet, but she was also happy to be going back home.

Bryce parked the car and rushed around to open her door for her. It was as if they were back to their first date. He offered her his hand and she took it. He helped her out of the car and led her to the front door. He opened the door but before she could walk in he swept her off her feet and carried her through the doorway like he had done the first day of their marriage. Zia loved the extra attention and effort. She giggled as he carried her up the stairs and to the bedroom.

He sat her down on the edge of the bed then bent down on one knee. He carefully slid off her shoes. She hadn't gone back to wearing heels yet so he had to undo the laces before he could remove her shoes. He stood up and brought his face close to hers until their foreheads were touching.

"You sit here and rest your feet," he whispered while looking into her eyes. "I'll go draw you a warm bath to relax in. I haven't done that in a long time."

Bryce disappeared for a few moments while Zia sat down on the bed. She wanted to collapse on the bed and fall asleep but she was also excited to have a bath. It'd been a while since she'd sat in a warm bath and relaxed. Her phone in her bag vibrated. She quickly checked it hoping it wasn't an email from her stalker to ruin her night. She sighed in relief when she saw it was a text from Willem.

"Congratulations on winning today. I didn't see you come out of the court, hope you got home alright. We need to celebrate sometime. Let me know when and I can set something up."

A smile pulled at the corner of her mouth, she didn't even realize it was there. Willem made her feel warm inside. It scared her thinking that someone else besides Bryce made her feel that way.

Bryce popped his head into the room and she dropped her phone onto the bed. He took her hand and led her down the hall to the bathroom. The air was filled with steam and the bath was overflowing with warm water and bubbles. The bath sat inside the double head shower so all the water that flowed out drained away.

Zia took a deep breath through her nose. The bubbles smelled of lavender and honey. Bryce made sure to use her favorite bubble bath and he used a lot of it. She was ready to jump straight in clothes and all.

She started unbuttoning her jeans but Bryce stepped in and took over. He undressed her slowly, leaving a gentle kiss behind on each of her body parts. She stood naked in front of him and he didn't blush or stare. She didn't expect him to. He had seen her naked hundreds of times since they got married.

"The bath is ready, my queen," Bryce said jokingly.

Zia's heart jumped into her throat and her blood turned cold from hearing that word. The only one whoever called her a queen was Baxter. The thought made her want to vomit.

"No, no, no," she stuttered, trying to find the right words to use. "Don't say that."

His brow furrowed and he stepped back from, and then a light bulb switched on in his head and his eyes widened with shock.

"Oh, I'm so sorry Zia," he said covering his mouth like a little boy who just swore for the first time. "Forget I said that, just enjoy the night, okay?"

It wouldn't be hard to forget a simple word. The difficult part was forgetting about Baxter. She hoped that once she completely destroyed Paradigm he would finally be out of her life.

Bryce helped her into the large tub and she sunk into the bubbles. More water overflowed but she didn't care. She stretched out her legs. She could feel all of her troubles flowing into the warm water and melting away. Her eyes were closed but she peeked through one to see Bryce turning around and leaving the room.

"Bryce," she said quickly to stop him from leaving. "Come and join me."

He didn't hesitate. She watched him undress and climb into the tub with her. She couldn't remember the last time she marveled at his chiseled, toned muscles. She loved how he wasn't too muscular but he was defined and worked on it. He did it all for her. She made a mental note to get back into shape for him.

The tub was more than big enough for the both of them. Bryce sat across from her and rubbed her feet. They talked, laughed, and the world seemed to disappear around them. Bryce stared into her eyes for the longest time and she stared back. She felt closer to him than she had felt in a long time and Bryce felt as if he would never lose her again. They washed each other and sat in the bath a little longer. Neither one of them wanted to leave this moment.

When the water grew cold, they had no choice but to leave. Bryce got up first and helped Zia exit the bath. He grabbed a towel big enough for the both of them and he dried her off, then himself, and wrapped it around them. He pressed his body into hers. She felt him harden against her pelvis and an itchy feeling returned inside her. She hadn't felt that feeling for a long time. She hasn't had the urge to have Bryce inside her for a very long time.

He stared straight into her eyes as if he were looking into her soul. He cupped her upper thighs and lifted her up. She wrapped her legs around his waist and her arms around his neck while he carried her to the bedroom. He grew harder and his tip rubbed against the lips of her vagina. The feeling made her body curl inwards and she bit her lip to stifle a moan escaping through her lips.

Bryce knelt on the edge of the bed and leaned forward, slowly lowering Zia onto the bed. He ripped the towel away from her body and threw it to the side. A tingling sensation shot through Zia's body as the tips of his fingers danced up the side of her thigh towards her breasts. He cupped her one breast in his hand and squeezed it gently. Zia was wet and ready for him but he wasn't done teasing her.

He kept his eyes on her the whole time. Not once did he look away. While his one hand was cupping her breast the other was dancing over her body. He dragged the tips of his fingers along the inside of her thigh and lightly touched the lips of her vagina. Her body twitched as he touched her there. She wanted more. She wanted to beg and moan for more but she let him take his time. He admired every inch of her with his hands but kept his eyes fixed on hers.

"I love you, Zia," he whispered as he leaned forward and kissed her.

His kiss was passionate and gentle, it seemed to last forever.

"I love you too," Zia felt as if she might have hesitated to reply but she didn't. It was true. After all they've been through, she really does love him.

He finally answered her desires and entered her. She gasped as his long, hard rod pushed inside of her. It felt better than she remembered. It made her body shudder and shake as his body rocked back and forth and he pulled and pushed in and out of her. Her vaginal juices coated his penis and he slid in and out easily. He didn't go in too deep or hold back. He gave her everything she could have asked for and more. Having Bryce touch her in this way made her feel like she was starved of love for years.

She dug her nails into the duvet and grabbed a handful of it. She moaned and groaned as the feeling inside her intensified. She wanted more and he gave it to her. He went deeper and faster. Their bodies moved in a perfect rhythm as she pressed her pelvis into him. He rubbed her G spot in just the right way, and it made her want to scream. He joined in on her moaning and he even growled. She hadn't heard that sound come out of his mouth in a long time. She liked it and she wanted more. Her vaginal muscles twitched and squeezed around his shaft.

"Oh Zia," he moaned.

The feeling built up until it was overflowing inside of her. She couldn't hold it in anymore. Her head dug into the bed and she arched her back pushing her pelvis further into him. She screamed as she climaxed and squeezed around his penis. Bryce growled loudly and collapsed on top of her body, but he didn't stop. He wasn't there yet. Every movement he made inside her was pure bliss and brought extreme ecstasy. He grabbed her hands and squeezed tight. He looked straight into her eyes as he climaxed. He emptied inside of her and she felt the hot liquid squirt into her. He twitched inside of her and let his body fully collapse on top of her.

He stayed inside of her but he didn't move. All his energy was gone and he just wanted to lay there and feel her pressed against his body. Zia let her body relax and she held his hand tightly in hers. They closed their eyes and let the moment last for as long as possible.

THE GLASS SHATTERED ALL OVER THE FLOOR AND THE sound was loud enough to wake up the whole house. It did wake up the whole house. The only people in the house were Zia and Bryce. Zia jumped up and threw the duvet off. She almost believed that the sound was another nightmare but Bryce was already up and out of the bed.

Zia could hear her heart beating in her ears and it drowned out anything Bryce was saying to her. She was sure he was saying something like, "stay here," but she was deaf to the outside world. All she could hear was her heart and the sound of glass shattering playing over and over in her mind.

Bryce put on his boxers and grabbed a metal bat he had hidden underneath the bed. Zia didn't even realize he had a bat hidden there. She watched him walk out the bedroom door. The moment he left her alone she felt vulnerable. Images of a man hiding under the bed or in the closet flashed through her mind. She imagined someone climbing through the window and attacking her while Bryce was downstairs investigating. She didn't want to stay here. She jumped out of the bed, threw her gown on, and followed him out of the room.

He was already at the bottom of the stairs when she reached the top. She looked down and gasped. There was a brick laying on the floor beside the front door surrounded by shards of glass from the window it had been thrown through. Bryce stood at the edge looking at it with his bat at the ready. Zia assumed he hadn't walked closer because he was barefoot and there was glass everywhere.

She walked down the stairs and peered at the brick. There was something tied to it. It looked like paper from where she was standing and she expected it might be another note from her stalker. She continued to the bottom of the stairs and walked past Bryce.

"Zia!" he exclaimed as she walked past him. "I told you to wait upstairs."

He tried to grab her arm but she was too far and he didn't want to step on the glass. He looked down and noticed Zia wasn't wearing any shoes either.

"Zia, you'll cut yourself. Come back here."

Zia didn't listen. She was in a trance and wanted to know what was tied to the brick. She tiptoed carefully through the glass shards, avoiding the big ones but still stepping on a few small ones. She didn't care. Something told her she needed to see what was attached to the brick.

She knelt down and untied the papers from the brick. Bryce watched helplessly from the side, unwilling to cut his feet open walking across to her. There was a single note on top of the stack of papers and she read it:

"You should have learned your lesson by now. You can't trust anyone."

She moved the note aside and unfolded the papers beneath it. They were all black and white copies of photos. Tears welled up in Zia's eyes and there was an ache in her chest as her heart broke. The pictures were of Bryce and Jazmine together. This time she knew exactly where the photos were taken and when. She knew that couch Jazmine was lying on because she had laid there once before with Bryce on top of her. The couch was in Bryce's office. There was a knot in her stomach and a foul taste in her mouth. She looked at the clothes they were wearing. They were both wearing those same clothes that day she found out about the will, the day she was pushed down the stairs and lost the baby.

Zia didn't know what to do. She thought that Bryce truly loved her, and maybe he did, but how can she love him when he lies to her face and cheats behind her back. She cheated on him but she did her best to become a faithful and worthy wife. Bryce hasn't been faithful, and she had a feeling that he never was. He might love Zia, but it's clear that he desires Jazmine as well.

Zia stood up, spun round, and threw the photos at Bryce, but she kept the note in her hand. The anger swelled up inside of her and threatened to blow up. All she could do was burst into tears and run past him. She ran up the stairs into the bedroom, closed and locked the door behind her. She didn't know what to do. So many thoughts raced through her mind and she wasn't sure which ones to act on. She knew one thing for certain, she needed to get out of there. She needed to get away from Bryce.

She couldn't call her parents, not at three in the morning, and if her father found out she was afraid, he would get into a fight with Bryce. There had to be somewhere else she could go. There had to be a bridge she hadn't burnt yet. She could barely breathe as she grabbed her phone and called the only person she knew would help her.

Bryce banged on the door and begged Zia to open it so he could explain. She wanted to open the door. She wanted to believe that all of those photos were faked. She just couldn't allow herself to be that blind anymore.

She knew on the day that something was wrong. She knew it was strange that Bryce had the door to his office locked and that he didn't want her to come in. He was holding the door closed for a reason, and now she knew what that reason was. She felt angry enough to grab that bat and hit Bryce with it, but she was also scared. If she couldn't trust Bryce, who could she trust?

Her phone vibrated and she grabbed her bag and headed for the door. She froze for a moment. She'd never breathed so deeply in all her life but right now she needed to be calm and strong. When she felt strong enough, she unlocked the door and stepped out.

"Finally," Bryce sighed. He was leaning against the hallway banister outside the door. "Zia, can we just talk about this?"

"There's nothing to talk about Bryce," Zia tried to sound calm and emotionless, even though she wanted to scream and yell at him. "I'm leaving now and I don't want you to follow."

She walked down the stairs but Bryce was quick on her heels.

"You're not thinking straight. Where are you going to go at four in the morning, huh?" Bryce jumped a few steps so he could reach the bottom before her. He stood in front of her blocking her way to the door. "Zia, I insist you go back upstairs, and we can talk about this. I'm not going to let you walk out of the house this early in the morning when it's clear that your judgment is impaired."

Her jaw fell open and the storm replaced the calm. Her eyes blazed, her cheeks turned red, and her lips curled into a scowl.

"Excuse me! My judgment at this moment is not been impaired. In fact, this is probably the smartest thing I have done in a long time. If anything, I would say my judgment was impaired when I let you drive me here and fuck me!" She pushed him out of the way and headed towards the front door. "I trusted you Bryce, and no matter what you tell me or what you tell yourself, my trespasses are nowhere near as horrible as yours. I was faithful our entire marriage, but you were never faithful. Were you?"

Bryce stayed silent, he just stared at her. Zia shook her head at him and turned to the front door. She opened it up and Willem was standing on the other side.

"Oh," he looked from Zia to Bryce and back to Zia. "Hello. Are you ready to go?"

"You're going with him?" Bryce raised his voice and for a moment Zia was shocked. "No! No, I won't allow this."

"Then it's a good thing I wasn't asking for your permission."

Zia stepped out of the house as Willem turned to walk to his car. Before Zia could follow Bryce launched through the doorway and grabbed her arm to pull her back.

"Bryce let go of me!"

"I'm not just going to let you drive off with some stranger at four in the morning."

Willem turned his head and the moment he saw what Bryce was doing he sprang into action. He launched at Bryce and ripped his hand off of Zia's arm. He then gently pushed Zia away from him and positioned himself in between her and Bryce.

"Get your hands off of my wife," Bryce growled at him.

Zia had never seen him act this way and it scared her. It was as if she was seeing his true face and up until now he had been wearing a mask to hide it.

"I don't care if she is your wife or just some random woman you just met," Willem said with a proud and confident voice. "A man should never touch a woman in the way you just touched Zia."

Bryce stepped toward him and even though Willem towered over Bryce, he lacked a little in the muscles department. Zia didn't want them to fight. She didn't want either of them to get hurt over her. She grabbed Willem's hand and pulled him back.

"Willem just leave it!" She begged him. "Can we please just get out of here?"

Willem would have gladly taken on Bryce to defend Zia's honor. He convinced himself that Bryce probably deserved any beating he was willing to give, but he was a gentleman and he wouldn't start a fight in front of a lady. He looked Bryce up and down one last time before turning away. He took Zia's hand and led her to his car. They climbed in the car and drove away. Zia didn't even want to look back. She was sure Bryce would jump into his car drive after them but she wouldn't risk looking back to make sure he didn't.

"Don't worry Zia, I'm going to take care of you." Willem reached his hand across and gently touched her hand. Her first instinct was to pull away but he pulled away first. "Tell me where you want to go and I'll take you there. Tell me what you want to do and I'll do everything in my power to help you do it."

Maybe it was the stress and anxiety speaking, but only one thought came into Zia's mind. There was only one thing she wanted to do right now. Willem could help her do it and he would. It was such an easy thought to have but she knew it wasn't going to be an easy thing to do.

"I just want to go home."

IF DESPAIR AND DEPRESSION HAD A SMELL, THEN ZIA'S childhood bedroom would reek of it. The curtains were shut all the time and the door was only opened whenever her mother or father walked in to check if she was okay or give her some food. Willem came to check on her constantly. He would sit at the edge of the bed and talk to her about nonsensical things.

"I saw a kitten today," Willem told her as she hid beneath the duvet covers. "It was the fluffiest creature I have ever seen. I would have adopted it and brought in home myself. However, I'm sure if I did, my own cat would have a thing or two to say about it."

Zia poked the top of her head out to look at Willem.

"You have a cat?" She muttered, her voice muffled by the folds of the duvet.

"Oh yes I do, her name is Muffin, and she loves to travel. That's good for me since my profession has me jumping from country to country. I always make sure to find a hotel that allows animals. She usually sleeps on the master bed all day while I work, then she'll demand I feed her the moment I get home. She's royalty, you know, or at least she thinks she is so don't tell her otherwise."

Zia couldn't help but let out a soft giggle and she smiled for the first time in ages. This warmed Willem's heart, knowing that he could make her happy even for just a moment. Zia pushed the duvet away from her face and sat up slightly. She was still in her winter pajamas and her hair was a bushy mess. Willem didn't seem bothered. He stared at her with bright, wide eyes as if he was looking at a lost kitten that needed to be saved. Then his smile faded as he realized that even now she was still an unavailable woman.

"Look Zia, I know that you don't want to do this, but you need to agree to a meeting with Bryce," he calmly explained. "You can't ignore him for the rest of your life. You two are still married and I can tell that you still love him. I think it's worth trying to work it out."

Zia sighed and the small smile she had a moment ago disappeared.

"If I agree to meet with him, I'm not sure what I will do. He's a different man. He's never grabbed me the way he did that night. He's never raised his voice the way he did to you."

"Stress changes people Zia, you should know that," Willem shuffled around so he could look straight at her without craning his head to the side. "Remember that you're not the only one that lost the baby. Bryce lost him too. That loss must have hit both of you really hard. After losing his child, it's understandable that Bryce doesn't want to lose you too."

After quickly weighing all of her options, Zia realized she had no choice. She can't leave any of this behind her if she continues to pretend none of it is happening. She must face it head on or say goodbye. Despite everything she's been through, she wasn't ready to say goodbye to Bryce.

"You're right," she eventually said. "I'll call him and set up a meeting. I would like you to drive me there, if you don't mind, just in case I need someone to bail me out."

Willem smiled and nodded his head. Zia was glad to have a friend like him in her life, after losing Jazmine who was her only friend not too long ago.

Willem said goodbye and left Zia to do what needed to be done. He made sure to hug her mother and shake her father's hand on the way out. Zia loved how he got along with her parents as well. Only after he left did Zia pick up her phone and message Bryce. He'd been calling and texting her non stop since the night she left him standing by the front door. She'd ignored all of them. She could only hope now that it's not too late and that he won't ignore her.

"We need to talk," she started her text but it sounded too formal so she erased it and started again. She can't believe she'd forgotten how to talk to her husband. "I need to talk to you, can we meet somewhere?"

She wasn't entirely happy with that text but it was better than the last one. She pressed send and it was too late to change her mind. Her phone vibrated from the reply almost instantly, as if Bryce was clutching his phone just waiting for her to text him.

"I need to talk to you too. Let's meet at the park we used to take Bugs to. I miss that park."

Zia smiled. She missed that park too. She replied agreeing to it and setting up a time to meet. Then she messaged Willem telling her what time to pick her up and where they were going. Now all Zia had to do was get out of bed and rejoin the land of the living. She hadn't had a proper shower in days and she was ready to feel the warm water run down her back.

Willem gave her a pep talk the whole ride to the park. Zia was nervous at first but as they entered her old neighborhood, she felt like she was home again. She remembered the trees as they drove past. She rolled down the window to smell the salt air she used to breathe in every day. She knew the streets, she knew the houses, and she knew the people walking down the street. She'd never really talked to any of them, but she would always say hello when passing them on her walk.

They turned the corner and she knew they were getting close to the park. Willem parked the car and Zia spotted Bryce sitting on the bench. It was the same bench they used to sit on while Bugs ran up and down. The same bench they would be sitting on while discussing whose turn it was to clean up after Bugs. Zia didn't think she would feel so emotional from seeing a bench.

She asked Willem to stay in the car and then she walked across the park. The moment Bryce saw her, his eyes lit up and he stood to greet her. He wanted to run across the park and embrace her, but he knew he couldn't. She would push him away. He stayed by the bench and waited for her to come to him. When Zia finally reached the bench she didn't know what to do. Bryce was standing right in front of her and a thousand thoughts and feelings raced through her mind. She wasn't sure which ones to act on.

Without warning she raised her hand and slapped it right across Bryce's cheek. It was a shock to both Bryce and Zia. She wasn't sure why she did it, but it made her feel a bit better. Bryce cradled his red, burning cheek in his hand. It was made far more painful by the winter chill in the air.

"I suppose I deserve that," he muttered. "I guess it won't hurt at all if I say I'm sorry."

"It might," Zia said while shrugging her shoulders. "You'll never know until you give it a try."

"Zia," he took a deep breath, "I'm sorry."

Zia didn't actually think that would work and neither did Bryce, but it turns out that was all Zia needed to hear. She launched forward and threw her arms around Bryce's neck. He wrapped his arms around her waist, lifted her up, and pulled her into his body. Their bodies melted together and fought off the winter chill. Tears rolled down Zia's cheeks and landed on the back of Bryce's shirt. Tears welled up in his eyes too. The hug lasted only a few moments but to the both of them it was an age of healing and love between them.

Bryce released his arms and lowered Zia to the ground. He took her hand and they sat down on the bench. Zia leaned against him and placed her head on his shoulder.

"You were right," Bryce said. "I love you, but I desired Jazmine. I don't know why but I couldn't help myself. We used to be in a relationship a long time before I even met you."

Zia bit her tongue. She already knew that after seeing that video her stalker sent her, but she wasn't about to tell him that. She kept quiet and listened to what he had to say. She didn't want to hear about Jazmine any more than she needed to, but she figured this was important for them to move forward.

"Our relationship wasn't a healthy one," Bryce continued. "We were both rich and powerful. Our relationship was purely a sexual one, but it was also abusive. She would go out with other men to make me jealous and I would do the same just to get back at her. I think that's what she wanted. She got off from it. She always wanted things that she couldn't have and when I went out with other girls to get back at her it was like a challenge for her to get me back. I wanted out. I needed a healthy, stable relationship. I needed to find a girl that I could marry, have a family with, and grow old with. I left her and hid myself." Bryce sighed and looked at Zia. "That was when I met you, that first day at Fargo Tower. I knew that Jazmine owned Spark and that it was situated in Fargo Tower so I thought that was the perfect place to hide from her, right under her nose. Little did I know that she actually worked there for some reason. The moment I saw her it was like those sexual desires came back. They were stronger than ever and I couldn't fight them." Bryce pushed off the bench and got down on his knees in front of Zia. He held her hand in his and looked in her eyes. "I love you Zia. I loved you then and I love you now. Every single time I let Jazmine take advantage of my sexual desires I felt horrible inside. I felt like you deserved someone better than me, someone more loyal and faithful. When you left that night I realized that I was blaming

Jazmine for my betrayal of you, when I should be blaming myself. I am the one who lost control and slept with Jazmine. I'm the one that needs to change. Zia, I am willing to change for the love you bring into my life. I don't want to lose you and I swear to you right now that Jazmine is out of our lives for good from this moment on."

Zia smiled and the tears poured down her cheeks like a storm. She didn't know what to say. She was happier in this moment than she had ever been in her whole life. She knew it was possible now. She and Bryce could move forward, try to start a family again, and live their lives together until they both grew old. That's all she wanted. That is what she was going to get no matter what.

Chapter
THIRTEEN

THE MOVERS WERE PROFESSIONALS AND THE BEST THAT money could buy. They not only carried everything into the house but they unpacked the furniture and placed it anywhere Zia asked them to. Then they moved it again to where Zia's mom preferred it. Zia has walked into the lounge twice now to see that the couch has been moved to a different spot.

"Mom," Zia called out and her mother rushed in from the kitchen. "Please stop telling the movers to rearrange the furniture. We can rearrange it ourselves when we're done."

"Okay dear, sorry, I'll leave them alone." She disappeared back into the kitchen but Zia was sure she'd be back to move the couch again.

Zia asked for this when she bought a house with a big garden house attached to the back and asked her parents to move in there with her. It was the least she could do for them. They had raised her and taken care of her during those few weeks she was fighting with Bryce. Now they didn't have to pay rent on a small, crappy house and could live with her in this big one. As a bonus she wouldn't be alone. Zia was still terrified to be left alone in the house at all after the things she's been through. She was convinced her stalker would throw another brick through the window or send her more dead bodies. She would never get any sleep if she was alone.

That's why she wanted to move. She wanted to sell the house that she and Bryce had been living in and move back to her old neighborhood. Somewhere she might be safe, even for just a little while. Bryce was happy to start their life from the beginning and he was even happier to have Zia's parents move in with them. The decision was made, the house was sold and things moved quickly from there.

Zia instructed the movers as to where to place her furniture but she eventually left it to her mother. She wasn't used to people doing what she said. She wasn't used to having enough money to pay people to do what she said. Now she had enough money to buy her own house, big enough for her and her parents to live in with a pool and garden. She had a lot of money after her book deal with Chiseled Bone and after marrying Bryce. Now she had all of that money plus what Baxter had left her in his will.

"How's it going?" Willem's voice made her jump but then she sighed and smiled when she looked at him.

"It's going great," she replied with the biggest smile he'd ever seen on her face. "You were right, the house is perfect and I think my mother is having the time of her life in there."

"I'm glad you like it," Willem reached out to Zia's face and tucked a loose tuft of hair behind her ear. "I'm glad to see you smiling again."

Zia's cheeks felt warm and his touch sent a tingling feeling through her belly, like tiny butterflies fluttering around. He stared into her eyes and she stared back. She quickly pulled her eyes away from him and turned her attention back to the house. The smile slowly faded away. Willem lowered his hand and his own smile disappeared along with hers, as if he couldn't be happy if she was sad.

"Let me take you out somewhere," Willem suggested but Zia immediately shook her head. "Come on Zia, it's been a whole year since you won the legal battle and separated Weingart and Paradigm. We still haven't celebrated that victory like I promised we would."

"I'm just too busy to do anything right now," Zia said and started walking away.

Willem followed after her, "I'm sure the movers will be done by tonight, and your parents will be more than happy to have the house to themselves for the night."

Zia walked into the kitchen where her mother was and leaned against the counter. Willem stood on the other side and leaned over, placing his hand gently on hers. Zia let it rest there for a moment but then pulled away. Bryce had gone back to his parents for a few days to sort out some things with his inheritance. Zia wasn't ready to let her faith fail because he wasn't around.

"Please Zia, let me treat you to dinner tonight," he insisted. "You deserve it after all."

Before Zia could answer or even think about it her mother spoke up and answered for her.

"Go with the man Zia!" She instructed. "If the man were begging you anymore he would be down on his knees right now. Stop denying the man, put on a sexy dress, and let this man treat you the way you deserve to be treated. I'm sure Bryce wouldn't mind you going out for a simple dinner."

Willem couldn't help but laugh and Zia couldn't either. The beaming smile returned to her face and she looked up at Willem.

"Okay then," she finally agreed. "Come back later tonight to pick me up, and I expect to be pleasantly surprised by whatever you have planned."

Willem picked up her hand and gently kissed the back of it. Zia felt the urge to pull her hand away again but she ignored it.

"Trust me, you will be," he said before bowing his head slightly to both her and her mother and leaving.

"Where do you find them Zia," her mother asked when Willem left, "and where can I find one."

"Mom!" Zia cried out more embarrassed than shocked. "You're married."

"So are you!"

ZIA CALLED BRYCE BEFORE WILLEM ARRIVED TO PICK HER up. They both talked about their days and Bryce asked her how moving into the new house is going. Zia explained her day and how her mother is taking full control of the furniture arrangements. Zia enjoyed talking to him and she wished she didn't have to hang up. She decided not to mention her dinner with Willem tonight. It would just upset him for no reason. She had said goodbye and hung up by the time Willem arrived.

She was glad that she dressed fancy because Bryce had taken her to the fanciest restaurant she had ever seen. She still wasn't used to living the rich life. This was the kind of place that rich people go to eat food covered in gold shavings that cost more than a car. This was the kind of place that Zia could probably afford to go but she never actually would.

Zia and Willem were led to their table and sat down. While Willem ordered them a bottle of champagne for the table, Zia looked around. She was reminded of her first date with Bryce. Everyone looked at her as if she didn't belong. That was because she was the only woman of color in the room. She had gotten over that feeling. If people want to stare then they can stare. Zia didn't care what other people thought of her anymore.

They ordered their food, popped the champagne and the night began. Zia could hardly touch her food. She was too busy staring at Willem and studying him. He is incredibly gorgeous. Zia always wondered why men like him are single. What is it in life that they're looking or waiting for, but haven't found?

"You don't like your food?" Willem asked, noticing her lack of eating.

Zia gasped and her cheeks turned a slight pink.

"Oh yes. It's delicious, thank you." She replied stuffing a sautéed mushroom into her mouth and hoping he wouldn't notice her blushing.

He was now the one not eating his food and staring at her. She wondered how long he planned to do that.

"You seem preoccupied. Is something on your mind?" he asked her.

"Your naked body," the thought popped into her head and she immediately regretted having it.

"Just work really."

"Well, let's talk about it. Otherwise, it'll distract you and steal your personal time. I've learned that in life."

Zia smiled at his simple truth while concocting a lie to tell him.

"I was just thinking about Paradigm," she finally said. "I think it needs a lot more than just a complete makeover, and I've got some big plans for it."

Zia wasn't lying because she had been thinking about that lately. The company's fraud charges had been dealt with and the company had been torn to the ground. However, with all the contacts the company has it is still very profitable and powerful in the right hands. All one needed to do was build it up from the ground and restart it. Zia had different plans for it though.

"Oh really, what are you planning? What could be more effective for it than a restructuring?"

"Demise."

Willem was in the middle of sipping on his champagne but Zia's reply nearly made him choke on it. He put the glass down, took a deep breath, and looked up at Zia.

"I don't want to assume what you're insinuating. Care to elaborate?"

"Maybe it's time to see it go. Maybe Paradigm is a dinosaur of the past and it needs to be buried with the rest of the fossils."

"Do you have any idea what Paradigm is worth? What it could be if it fell into the wrong hands?"

People truly care more about money and power than they do about any person. They only care about what they can possess. How much they can withhold from others and keep for themselves. They are devils in disguise being worshipped as kings. Dwight was one, and Zia had no plans to become one herself. She thinks of herself as the anti. She wants to see Paradigm go, she has no intentions of letting it go, but she decides not to correct Willem on this. She has plans in place. She'll see them through until the very end if she has to.

"I know exactly what it's worth in every way besides the mere financial face value," Zia informed him. "I have no intention of ever allowing any other person to own it."

He squints his eyes at her as the wheels in his mind turn. Zia refuses to discuss it further with him. At this moment she doesn't fully trust him anymore. He did used to work for Baxter after all.

"You're the boss," he said, raising his glass to her before taking a sip.

That she is. She still wasn't used to being the boss, but no matter how close she has gotten to Willem over these past few months, no matter how much of a friend she sees him as, she pays his bills, which makes her his boss. That's the simple truth of it. She had to keep that in mind when talking business with him. She didn't want him to get the wrong impression or think that he has more power than he actually does. Zia was reminded of those days when she was a simple, innocent chameleon, adapting to survive in a world that would devour her. She's evolved since then. She is now a ravenous snake, slithering across the ground and devouring the chameleon she used to be.

Zia watches him closely as he slices into his filet mignon, seductively sliding the juicy meat into his mouth, guiding it with his tongue. His lips linger on the fork much long then necessary. His dreamy blue eyes pierce her veneered composure. She could deny this moment, but she couldn't see a reason to.

With her humanity effectively muted, the sight of Willem's rippling, heaving chest awakens and scorches her lower parts, without objection. His perfect gleaming smile provokes her sinister grin. She's unsure how to be the aggressor, but she knows one thing is true; she wants him, even if she can't have him.

Her vaginal nectar seeps into the crotch of her panties. His flirtatious glances remind her of times where she was innocent. Those times are long gone now.

She cleared her throat to break the silent stare between them.

"I'm a bit tired. I think I should be heading back home now."

"No dessert?" Willem seemed intent on making her stay longer, as he leans across the table.

"I think there's some ice cream at the house, I'll just have some of that."

"Why don't you come up to my room for a little while?" He used his fork to gesture upwards. "I've got chocolates and sweets up there, and I'm sure I've got a bottle of whiskey too."

Zia's eyes followed his fork, "Your hotel is above the restaurant?"

He nodded, "I find it extremely convenient and also they have the best room service in the city. Well, what do you say?"

Zia hesitated, but something inside of her was burning to go up with him. It couldn't hurt if she went up for a little while. She was an adult and she was in charge of her life, why should she hesitate when a friend asks her to his room for a drink?

"I'm sure it will be fine if I come up for a little while," she responded, "but then I must really get going. I can't leave my mother alone to rearrange the household unsupervised. The couch might wind up in the kitchen."

Willem chuckled and a bright, gleaming smile remained on his face while he called for the bill. With intent pouring from his eyes, he pays the bill, and they head up to his room.

He led her to the elevators at the back of the restaurant that leads up to the hotel rooms. He pressed the button for his floor and the doors slowly pushed closed. As soon as the elevator doors close, her pheromones apparently scatter because he moves closer. The magnetism is undeniable. They face each other and he leans into her. His erection caresses her thigh. Their lips graze. Desire oozes from their pores. Just as she throws caution to the wind, they reach his floor and the doors open.

They walk down the hall, Willem leading her to his room. With each step she takes she wants to turn back and head home, but with each step she desires him more and wants to feel him inside of her. Her mind is at war with itself.

As soon as they walk through the door, his arms are around her waist from behind, embracing her tenderly and burying his face in her hair. He inhales her scent and kisses the back of her neck and shoulders. Zia trembles and gasps. His erection pressed into her back and throbbed against her. He wanted her just as much as she wanted him.

He moved his hand down her chest, in between her breasts, across her stomach, and down to her thighs. Tingles shoot up her spine and she closes her eyes. He uses his finger tips to lift her dress up and slips his fingers into her panties. She gasped and bit her lip as his fingers pressed against her clit and moved in a circular motion. His one arm was still wrapped tightly around her waist and holding her up. She leaned her head back and pushed into him as his fingers danced around her vaginal area.

She gasped, moaned, and tried hard not to scream out as he moved his fingers further down and pushed them inside of her. First only two fingers, then three fingers, he went in the last time with four fingers and the sensation weakened Zia's legs. She wanted more than that. She wanted all of him inside of her. He teased her further, playing with her clit faster and pushing against it harder. The feeling was building up inside of her. He was going to take her there before even entering her and she didn't want to stop him.

She leaned her head back and prepared to scream out as she climaxed but an image flashed into her mind before she could. As the feeling built up inside of her and threatened to explode, the image of Bryce's face popped into her head. He was looking at her with a loving and innocent smile. Her eyes snapped open and she pulled away from Willem. She stumbled forward and collapsed on the ground. She couldn't breathe and just looked up at him with a horrified look on her face. She was horrified with herself. How could she have done this? How could she have been so willing to betray her husband so soon after finally healing their relationship? They had only just begun to build it up from the ground and she was seconds away from destroying it.

"What's wrong?" Willem asked her, the worry in his eyes dominated any feeling he might have had in the moment. "Did I hurt you?"

"I can't do this Willem," Zia gasped, huffed, and puffed as she pulled herself off the ground and fixed her dress. "I'm married to Bryce! I love him and I'm not going to destroy him like this. Not again. I might have a desire for you, but I have no love for you Willem. I love Bryce, and that is stronger than any kind of desire." Zia pushed past him into the hall. "I need to go home."

Willem stood in the doorway for a few seconds then rushed out after her.

"Zia!" He called out as he raced her to the elevator. When he caught up with her he showed her his car keys. "Let me drive you. It's late and it's too dangerous to be prowling the streets looking for a cab."

Zia looked him up and down. She didn't want to be in a room with him any longer but she agreed that she didn't want to be wandering around the streets looking for a cab. She remembered the last time she did something like that in New York. It didn't go well. She nodded her head in agreement and he followed her into the elevator.

He watched her from a distance. It was driving him crazy, having to keep his distance and stay away from her. He wanted to touch her. He wanted to take her away from all of these peasants who were beneath her and raise her up like the queen she is. They would both sit on their thrones beside each other one day. He would be the king and she would be his queen. They would rule the new world with a father's iron fist and a mother's open heart.

That day was near but he needed to be patient and wait for her to come to him. His plans to pull her away from the people she loves and break her trust in them failed. That didn't matter. There were other ways to break the bonds she has formed. The baby was already dealt with and the annoying mutt was out of the way. His next target would be her family. A queen is unable to rise above her subjects if there are things holding her down.

*T*HE DRIVE WAS SILENT AND UNCOMFORTABLE. ZIA wished they hadn't driven so far away from her home in the first place, then this drive wouldn't have been such a long one. She wanted to tell him how sorry she was but she couldn't bring herself to talk. At least she didn't want to talk about the events of the evening. She would rather forget that the night happened at all, but she knew it wouldn't be that easy. She had betrayed Bryce in some way and she would never forgive herself for it. Bryce didn't need to know though, because it wasn't going to happen ever again.

"Zia," Willem spoke up but she cut him off the moment he spoke her name.

"Willem don't! We don't need to speak. We don't need to say anything okay. Just forget that anything ever happened and you and I can try and get back to our normal lives."

"Okay," he took a deep breath. "Can we talk about something? This drive is becoming increasingly boring and awkward, and we still have at least 30 minutes left before we reach your house."

Zia sighed. He was right. It was getting extremely boring and awkward the longer they tried to pretend the other wasn't in the car. They needed to talk about something. She wasn't sure what to talk about though. A thought crossed her mind. It seemed like a crazy one at first but she thought it could at least make for interesting conversation.

"You used to work for Baxter, right?" Zia asked him. If she were to allow Willem to work for her further, she needed to know more about his loyalty. She had spent too long thinking of him as her friend. She was finished with openly trusting people.

"Sorry? Oh, you mean Dwight. Yes, I used to work for him. I was one member of his considerably large legal team."

"How close were you to him?"

"Not too close at all," he braked slightly as they took the next corner. "The first time I was alone in a room with him was when he changed his will to include you. Up until that point I had only ever been given instructions that came from him through other people."

Zia smiled slightly. She was feeling a little bit more comfortable having Willem around now. If he barely knew Baxter then there was very little chance he was still loyal to him. She could rest easy now.

"I was pretty close with his family at one stage," Willem added and Zia's blood turned cold.

"His family? Are you talking about Jazmine and his wife?"

Willem shook his head, "No, I didn't know them. I'm talking about his mother, sister, and brother."

Zia's mind was spinning wildly. Of course Baxter had a family, why was this a surprise to her? She figured that thinking of his family made him seem more human and less like a monster. Then a memory hit her in the face like a brick. She remembered everything that Dr. Herb has been teaching her. She closed her eyes for a second and entered the safe place in her mind. She left her office and ran down the hallway of doors. When she found the right door she didn't hesitate to step in.

She remembered meeting Detective John in a hotel room in New York all that time ago. Back when Jazmine was her friend and she could trust her with everything. She remembered the Detective mentioning something about Dwight having a family. A mother and sister. He mentioned how he thought that Dwight was the one behind their deaths.

"Wait," she thought to herself. "He only mentioned a mother and a sister. He said nothing about Dwight having a brother."

She opened her eyes and exited her mind. Willem was looking at her like a frightened puppy in the corner.

"Did you just say that Baxter had a brother?" she asked him, ignoring the way he was looking at her.

"Y-yes," he stuttered, glancing at the road in front of them and back at her. "He had a little brother. They were born two years apart, but they looked like they could have been twins. They even sounded the same sometimes."

All the pieces clicked together in Zia's head and everything started to make sense. The picture her stalker sent her of the two boys that looked like two young Baxters. That must have been Baxter and his little brother when they were young. The voice on the phone call she received when she got back from the hospital. It sounded just like Baxter, but it couldn't have been because he was dead, but Zia would bet everything that she has that his brother is alive and well. What if Baxter's brother has the same beliefs and plans for Zia that Baxter did? Zia turned ice cold and her chest tightened. Her heart was now in her stomach and her mind jumped all over the place.

"How far are we from my house?" She asked him. Suddenly she was really anxious to get home.

"About 20 more minutes," he replied.

"Can you go a little faster please? I really need to get home right now."

Willem rushed Zia home as fast as he could without breaking any traffic laws. Her mind was racing with too many thoughts for her to handle. She was sure that her stalker was Baxter's younger brother. He must be the one sending all of those emails, he's the one that was outside her house that day, he's the one that kidnapped Bugs and delivered him back to her in a box, and he's the one that called her the day she got back from the hospital. He did all of it. She figured that much out. Now all she had to do was figure out why Baxter's little brother is determined to tear her life apart.

She had a bad feeling that he was just getting started and she needed to get home straight away. It was still a new house so she couldn't tell if she was getting close or not. Eventually she saw it in the distance. Willem stopped in front of the house and Zia jumped out of the car.

"Are you going to be okay?" Willem asked her, but Zia had already slammed the door closed and was heading towards the house.

Willem sighed. There was no point in him trying any longer. He put the car in gear and drove away. He didn't think he'd see Zia again.

All the lights in the house were off and it almost looked abandoned. She thought that perhaps her parents had already gone to bed. She changed her mind considering she'd never known them to do that as early as 9pm. She put her key in the door but it was already unlocked. A lump formed in her throat and her heart dropped to the pit of her stomach. She was frozen to the spot but she forced herself to push forward.

She twisted the handle slowly and hoped it wouldn't make too much noise as she opened the door. The door didn't squeak and she was able to make a silent entrance. She let out a soft sigh of relief. It was pitch black inside and she wasn't entirely sure where the light switches were, so she reached into her purse and pulled out her phone. She moved forward slowly, using the flashlight on her phone as her guide.

She first scanned the walls looking for the nearest light switch. She found one across the room from her. She flipped it but nothing happened. Memories of the day she was pushed down the stairs at FFLL flashed in her mind. Whoever pushed her down the stairs was able to turn the power to the building off so she couldn't use the elevator. She was afraid that once again the power had been cut and someone in the house was waiting to take advantage of it.

Her next thoughts were for her parents. Where are they? Are they alright? Had someone come here to hurt them because of her? She swallowed the growing lump in her throat and forced herself to move further into the house. She needed to find her parents and get out of this house. She just hoped that she didn't arrive too late.

She avoided the stairs and searched the ground floor of the house first. As she entered each room her heart rate would rise and the sound of her heart beating would flood her ears. She found each room empty and left. She was determined to avoid the stairs for as long as possible so she checked outside in the garden and by the pool first. The electric pool cover was pulled across the pull and all the outside lights were off too. There was no one in sight here as well.

Zia sighed as she realized the only other place to check was the top floor. Zia would have to brave the stairs to continue her search for her parents. She would keep her guard up this time. No one was going to get the best of her and push her down the stairs in her own home.

She made her way toward the stairs and climbed them slowly, as she reached the top she immediately started her search of the top floor. Once again, she found each room empty. She had searched the whole house but it seemed as if it was empty and she was alone. Whoever was here and turned off the power was gone now. The question still burned in her mind; where have her parents gone?

She went back outside and did what she should have done when she first got here. She called her mother's phone. There was no answer and she couldn't hear it ringing in the house. She tried her father's phone but came up with the same result. A knot formed in her stomach and her chest tightened to the point where she couldn't breath. She collapsed on the steps that led up to the front door. She didn't know what else to do. Zia picked her phone back up and dialed the police.

HER NEW HOUSE IS FILLED WITH MEN IN UNIFORMS. THEY searched the whole house as she had done and told her they found no signs of break in or a struggle. Then they informed her that her parents were also nowhere to be found. Zia vibrated with anger because all they did was tell her what she already knew. She tried to call Bryce to let him know but he didn't answer. She figured he was busy so she left him a text.

"Mrs. Fink, shall we go through your statement again?" the police officer sitting on the couch opposite her asked. "That is if you're up to it."

Zia nodded, put down her phone, and gave him her full attention.

"You said you rushed home from a dinner date, saw that the lights were off and found that the door was unlocked. You entered the home, tried to turn on the lights but the power was off. Then you searched the house and when you couldn't find your parents you decided to call the police. Is that all correct?"

"It wasn't a date," Zia corrected him and he furrowed his brows at her.

"It was just dinner; it wasn't a date."

"Okay ma'am," he put his notebook away and stood up. "There doesn't appear to be any evidence of a break in and we can't say for certain that your parents are missing."

"They are missing!" Zia stood up to meet him but he still towered over her slight frame. "My parents would never just disappear without telling me and neither of them is answering their phones. Also, I didn't leave the door unlocked and neither would my parents. That's your evidence of a break in."

"Please, Mrs. Fink. I'm going to have to insist you calm down," he raised one hand in front of him and placed the other on his pepper spray.

"What are you going to do? Pepper spray me? You're at least 2 feet taller than me, do you consider me a threat?" Zia collapsed back on the couch and the tears poured from her eyes uncontrollably. "I just want you to find my parents."

"Captain!" one of the men outside by the pool called out and both Zia and the officer in front of her raised their heads to look at him. "Captain you need to come have a look at this."

The captain walked outside with the officer and Zia followed behind them. He led them past the pool and towards the house at the back of the garden. Zia didn't even think to look in there because the door was locked and they hadn't received the key from the landlord yet. Zia thought that he might have dropped the key off while she was with Willem and her parents started moving their stuff inside.

They all walked in and the place was turned upside down. Furniture was overthrown, lamps and vases were shattered on the ground, and some of the windows were broken. Zia gasped when she saw it. This was more than enough evidence to show that someone did break in and that her parents were attacked. She quietly sobbed into her hands. She couldn't bear to think what might have happened to them.

The Captain looked back at Zia and sighed.

"I'm sorry ma'am, but it looks like you were right." He walked past her back out into the garden. "Listen up men! It looks like we have a break in and possible kidnapping on our hands. I want a forensics team down here now. Nobody is to touch anything else from this point on." The men quickly went to work and he turned back to face Zia. "We'll do what we can, Mrs. Fink. We'll try to find your parents for you."

At that point Zia's phone rang in her pocket. It was Bryce and for a second, she didn't want to answer and tell him what happened, but she did.

Bryce hopped into the Weingart jet and flew home straight away. Zia asked that some police officers stay with her until Willem managed to get to the house. Zia was forced to wait outside while the forensics team did their job. They came in with their protective gear and covered every inch of her house. Zia was certain that they wouldn't find anything. She had a feeling that Baxter's brother was behind this, and he was probably just as smart as him and twice as dangerous. Baxter had tried to kill her mother, but he never kidnapped anyone. Zia couldn't help but wonder what game this guy was playing, and how he expected it to end.

Willem stayed with her until Bryce got home. The Weingart jet was faster than most commercial planes so it was only about a five-hour flight for him. He wasn't happy to see Willem but he dropped all of his hostility so he could comfort Zia. She collapsed in his arms and buried her face in his chest. She let it all out. All of the tears she'd been holding in since all of this started. The tears she wanted to cry when she lost the baby but she was too busy working on her revenge. The tears she needed to shed when she found out Bryce was sleeping with Jazmine but her anger took hold of her instead. Even the tears she held back when she saw Bugs' dead body. She let them all out. All Bryce could do was hold her tight and be there for her.

"It's okay Zee," Bryce whispered. "The police know what they're doing. They're going to find your parents."

"No, they won't!" Zia stuttered through the tears with a shaky voice.

"They won't find them. He won't let them."

"Who won't let them?" Willem stepped forward. His confused expression matched Bryce's.

"What are you talking about Zia?" Bryce asked her.

Zia sucked the remainder of her tears back and wiped her soaked cheeks with her sleeves. She took a few deep breaths until she was sure she wouldn't burst into tears the moment she spoke.

"I'm not entirely sure who he is, but he's been sending me emails for a while now," Zia explained. "I didn't say anything because I thought that he was just another crazy stalker at first. It started escalating quickly and by the time I realized he wasn't just another stalker it was too late to stop him."

"What has this guy done Zia?" Willem asked. "Do you think he's responsible for your parent's disappearance?"

Zia hesitated but she nodded her head in response.

"I'm sure he's also the one that killed Bugs and sent him back to me. At first, I thought it might have been Jazmine, but now I'm certain it was him. He's also the one that threw that brick through the window, and I think he pushed me down the stairs that night."

Bryce's mouth was hanging open and his eyes were squinted in confusion. His arms had gone limp and he wasn't holding onto Zia anymore.

"Wait, you thought that Jazmine was the one that kidnapped and killed your dog?" Willem asked and Zia just stared at him, wondering how that was the one thing that confused him.

Bryce spun around and shot a look at him that could only be described as a mix between confusion, hatred, and pure rage.

"She just told you this guy pushed her down the stairs causing her to have a miscarriage and has kidnapped her parents, and you're stuck on the damn dog!" Bryce yelled so loudly Zia's hand shot up to her ears to protect them. "Who is this guy Zia, I'm going to kill him."

Zia wasn't sure how she felt about this Bryce. She'd never seen that much rage in his eyes before. She liked how willing he was to protect and avenge her but she was scared that he was going to get himself hurt in the process. She told him this much. She decided that she should tell them both everything she knew.

"As I said, I'm not sure who he is, but I think he might be Baxter's brother," Zia explained. "In one of the emails he sent me an old picture. At first I thought it was of two young Baxters. I figured he'd edited it to make me think Baxter had a twin or just to mess with me.

"Last night Willem was telling me how much he knew about Baxter, I mean Dwight, and you mentioned that he had a younger brother."

Willem nodded, the wheels in his head turning once again, "Yes, he did. I remember seeing a picture of the two of them on his desk. He was fond of his brother. He loved him more than he did the rest of his family."

"What happened to his brother?" Bryce asked him. "Do you know where he is now?"

"No, nobody knows what happened to him. The rest of Dwight's family was killed in an accident, and after that his brother disappeared. It was like he dropped off the face of the earth. The only person who knew where he was, unfortunately, was Dwight."

"Jazmine might know!" Zia piped up as the thought popped into her head. "He was Jazmine's father. She might have known about his brother, and she might have kept in contact with him."

"Didn't Jazmine once say that she was Dwight's only living relative," Willem mentioned, which made Zia's smile disappear. "Why would she say something like that when she knew that his brother was still living? Unless she believed that there was no reason for him to contest the will, which meant that he was out of the equation."

"We can't spend all night debating this," Bryce said, taking charge of the situation. "Right now Jazmine is the only chance we have to find this guy. It's not going to hurt us to go ask her some questions."

"You're right," Willem agreed, grabbing his keys from his pocket. "I'll help in any way I can. We can take my car. Zia you should stay here and wait for me and Bryce to come back."

"I would prefer she come with us," Bryce interrupted him before Zia could agree or disagree.

"She will be safer here with the police than with us, don't you think?"

Zia realized she wasn't going to get a say here so she kept quiet while they worked it out. Bryce thought for a moment then nodded in agreement. He walked towards Zia and took her face in his hands. He leaned his head down and pressed his forehead against his. She felt the warmth of love flow from him into her.

"I'll be right back," he whispered. "I'll find your parents for you. I promise."

He kissed her and then turned to follow Willem to his car.

Zia sat helplessly on the porch steps as she watched Bryce and Willem drive away. She wished she could go with them, but she didn't want to see Jazmine. She was afraid she would slap her, or worse. Her thoughts of Jazmine aside, she also didn't want to be alone. Even with a house full of police behind her, Zia still felt alone. She didn't know any of them, and she certainly didn't trust them. Baxter was smart and she had to assume his brother was just as smart.

She sat there and shivered. She wanted to go inside but the police officers chased her out when she tried. She asked if one of them could bring her a blanket. He went inside and she waited for him to come back. She was still dressed in her short, tight black dress she wore to dinner with Willem. She was surprised Bryce didn't ask her why she was so dressed up. She figured he was preoccupied with the fact that her parents were missing to notice how she was dressed. She hoped Willem wouldn't say anything to him.

Zia's phone rang in her purse and she quickly rummaged through it. Bryce and Willem couldn't be at Jazmine's house already. Something was wrong and a knot formed in her stomach. She answered the phone without thinking or even looking at the caller ID.

"Bryce, is that you?" She cried frantically into the phone. "What's going on, are you at Jazmine's already?"

There was no immediate reply. All she could hear on the other end was heavy breathing. She pulled the phone away from her face and looked at the caller ID. It was her mom. Her eyes widened and her skin crawled with bumps. Slowly, she placed the phone back to her ear.

"Hello?" she whispered.

"Hello Zia," a voice replied. The voice sounded like Baxter, but she knew better than to think that. It was Baxter's brother.

"What do you want? Where are my mother and father? What have you done with them?" Zia had so many questions and she just wanted to yell at him. She wanted to jump through the phone and strangle him.

"You shouldn't have called the police, Zia. You shouldn't have called anyone. Now mommy and daddy are going to pay dearly for your insolence."

Zia's blood went cold when she heard her mother scream in the background.

"Wait! No! Stop it please!" Zia cried out. She couldn't stop the tears from pouring down her face.

She looked back as she remembered the house behind her was full of policemen. She could go in there and fetch one of them but how would that help? Baxter's brother would find out and hurt her parents, or kill them. She needed to keep this to herself. She stood up and walked away from the house so they couldn't hear her.

"What do you want from me?" She asked him. "I'll do anything you want me to, just don't hurt my parents please."

"That's more like it," he chuckled. "It is the place of a queen to obey her king. She must rise above those beneath her but remain below the man who owns her."

Zia swallowed hard. Baxter's brother is just as delusional as Baxter was, but somehow worse. He seemed to have different feelings towards Zia than Baxter did. She knew that deep down Baxter loved her, but this man seemed to only want to possess her and use her.

"This is just the start of it Zia," he continued. "Soon you will lose everything or willingly leave it behind. The choice is yours my queen. Give up this mundane life and come to me, so we can rule together. If you do not do as I say, I will take everything away from you until I am the only thing left in your life."

The line went dead. Zia stood there for a while longer and she wasn't sure what to do. The phone was frozen to her ear. She couldn't go to him, even if she knew where he was.

The officer she asked to bring her a blanket walked outside and handed it to her.

"Ma'am is everything alright?" he asked as he draped the blanket over her shoulders.

Zia didn't answer. She couldn't hear, move, speak, or think about anything except Baxter's brother. A monster had her parents and he was using them against her. He was using everything she had against her and she was helpless to stop him.

The officer remained by her side and waited for her reply. His concern painted plainly on his face. He was young. This was probably his first day on the job and he had no idea what to do.

The silence between them and in Zia's mind was interrupted by static from the officer's radio. He walked a little bit away from Zia and answered it. He turned the volume up, loud enough for Zia to hear. The man on the other end informed him of an accident not far from here. The ambulance is on its way and two men are injured. One was driving the car the other was in the passenger seat. They failed to break at a red light and drove head on into the side of a truck. The officer then went on to describe the car as well as the men inside it.

Zia gasped and snapped back around to look at the officer.

"That's Bryce and Willem!"

Chapter
SIXTEEN

She ran down the halls, her bare feet slamming silently against the cold tiles. The hospital was busy this time of night, nurses and patients rushing back and forth, and everyone was too busy to talk to her. She needed to find Bryce. She needed to know that he was okay, but no one had time to answer her questions.

The officer who was with her when she found out was kind enough to escort her to the hospital. While she searched the halls for her husband, he asked the nurses and doctors some questions. They were always willing to stop and answer when he showed them his badge.

"They're in the emergency ward," the officer told her and then gestured to a nurse beside him. "This nurse has agreed to take you to them. I have to get back to your house now before they realize I'm gone."

Zia was so overwhelmed with grief and gratitude she didn't know what to say. The tears were like a waterfall, blocking her vision. She jumped up and wrapped her arms around his neck.

"Thank you so much!" She said to him before giving him a kiss on the cheek and following the nurse down the hall.

The hospital seemed like it was made up of endless halls and multiple doors. It was a maze of sickness, bright lights, and cold tiles. She was glad to have a nurse lead the way or she might get lost for ages. They reached the emergency room and the nurse took her straight to the bed Bryce was in.

She threw the curtains back and gasped as she saw him. He was bruised and covered in cuts. He had blood on his face and wires and tubes protruding from his arm. His eyes were shut tight and both of them were black. She wanted to take his hand and squeeze it. She wanted to hug him and hold him, but she was afraid she would hurt him further, so she stayed away from him.

The nurse moved around the bed and grabbed the clipboard hanging beside it. She flipped through the pages. She nodded, hummed, and clicked her tongue as she read it.

"Your husband is going to be okay Mrs. Fink," she said as she put the clipboard back down. "From what I can tell the accident was bad but both he and the driver got lucky. He has a few broken ribs, a fractured clavicle, a dislocated knee, and he suffered a major blow to the head. He'll be kept unconscious for a few days as the swelling in his head goes down, but other than that there seems to be no other complications."

Zia listened to her carefully but everything she stated just made her want to run and hide. Everything she said sounded horrible. He looked bad but it sounded like he was worse. Before Zia knew it the nurse was by her side with her hand on her shoulder.

"He's going to be just fine," she whispered with a gentle voice. "Trust me, this is one of the finest hospitals in the city. He's in good hands, and the accident could have been a lot worse than it was."

Zia took in a deep breath and let it out slowly. She managed a smile while she wiped the tears from her eyes. The nurse looked her up and down, obviously noticing the very revealing dress she was wearing and how she was shivering.

"I'll go fetch you a blanket," she said. "If you want to see the driver, he's in that bed over there, and he's awake."

Zia followed the nurse's finger to the bed across the hall and thanked her. The nurse walked away, and Zia headed over to the bed where Willem was supposed to be. She pulled the curtain back slightly and slipped in. Willem looked up at her with a terrified look on his face.

"Oh," he sighed. "It's just you."

"Who were you expecting?" she asked him and glanced down at him quickly.

His leg was in a cast and elevated in some contraption. He had a few bandages around his head and his arms. He wasn't as banged up as Bryce but he wasn't in a good way either.

"Listen Zia, we don't have much time," he whispered. "He tried to kill us. Dwight's brother tried to kill us."

Zia suspected that he might be behind the accident but she hadn't been sure.

"How can you be certain?"

"I know he did it because Dwight used to do it." Willem sighed and lowered his head. "We knew about it, of course we did, we were his legal team. We were paid to keep him out of trouble and that's what we did no matter what. We knew that he was up to something, and we knew that his wife's car accident wasn't just a normal accident. We didn't say anything because that was our job." Willem tried to sit up further but he just grunted painfully and lied back down. "I tried to break Zia. I stomped on the brakes hard. They weren't working. That's how Dwight used to do it. He'd cut the brakes to the car so that the victim had no idea until it was too late. It will look like the car malfunctioned in some way if the police investigate. Whoever this guy is, he knows all of Dwight's tricks and that makes him even more dangerous than Dwight."

Zia's knees felt weak and she couldn't stand anymore. She sat down on the edge of the bed and let her head fall into her hands. It was too much to process. This monster has her parents and he tried to kill Bryce and Willem. How could she fix this? Was there even a way to fix this?

"Zia, I know you're probably scared," Willem continued, keeping his voice extra low this time. "You need to go back to my hotel room. The keycard is in my jacket by the side table. My laptop is in the top drawer on the right side of my bed. On my laptop there is a file hidden in the C drive titled 'Zia'. It's everything that Dwight wanted you to see. He gave it to me the day he rewrote his will and told me to give it to you when I thought you needed it."

"But why?"

Willem shook his head, "I don't know. I didn't understand it at first, but as I said before, I did my job no matter what. Maybe there's something in that file that can help you figure out who this guy is. Maybe there's something in there that can help. Dwight might have known this was going to happen and he wanted to prepare you for it. Dwight was smart and he would have done anything to keep you safe."

"I thought you said you didn't know him that well."

"I might have lied a bit about that. I knew him, but I didn't know the man that you knew. Go Zia, quick. Before this guy does something else."

Zia grabbed the keycard from Willem's coat and went back to Bryce before she left. She gave him a gentle kiss on the forehead and then left the hospital.

THE CAB DROPPED HER OFF AT THE HOTEL AND SHE rushed up to Willem's room. She wanted to move quickly but she didn't want to draw too much attention to herself. Baxter's brother could be watching her. She was sure that he'd been following her and watching her since the beginning. How else would he know as much as he did? How else would he have gotten those photos of Bryce with Jazmine in his office?

When she got to the room she double checked the door was locked behind her then searched the room to make sure it was empty. When she was certain she was alone, she fetched the laptop. It was exactly where Willem said it would be. She opened it up and did a search for the file named after her. When she found it she couldn't open it because it was password protected.

She grunted, "You could have mentioned the password, Willem," she mumbled to herself.

She tried several different words that Willem might have used but then she realized that it was Baxter's folder for her. There was only one password she could see him using for it. She typed in the word 'queen' and the folder opened up. It was filled with documents, images, and videos. She shuffled through them until she found something that might be helpful to her. She didn't have time to look at everything in the file. She found a document labeled NYC Psychiatric Institute. She opened that file up and read it as quickly as she could.

The document was a check out procedure from the institute and it had Dwight's signature at the bottom of it. Dwight wasn't the one that was checked out of the institute though. He checked out someone named Alexander. Zia put the document aside and continued searching through the file.

She found several more documents from the same facility and each one had Dwight's signature at the bottom and mentioned someone named Alexander. Zia wasn't sure who he was and why Baxter wanted to show these to her, but she couldn't wonder about that now. She needed to find something that could help her get this guy and save her parents.

She came across a video, she was going to scroll right past it but she recognized the face on the screenshot. It was Jazmine, and it looked like she was in the Fargo Tower building. Zia opened up the video and let it play.

The video started with Baxter's face, Zia never thought she would see it again. She forced herself to keep watching. He was setting up cameras and testing them. The single video feed split into several small ones, all of them showing a certain part of Fargo Tower. Baxter had surveillance cameras set up in Fargo Tower. She felt sick to her stomach, but she kept watching.

The footage was sped up and then slowed down again. It was night and Zia noticed the time stamp at the bottom corner. This footage was from the night that Baxter was killed. She spotted Jazmine on one of the video feeds sneaking into the building. Zia knew she was there that night, but she figured she came in after Baxter did. Judging by the time on the video, she had snuck in before Baxter even arrived, while Zia was still in her office reading Eve. She watched Jazmine sneak into the security room and turn off the building's surveillance cameras. Zia remembered that there was no video evidence of that night but she never thought anything of it. Jazmine turned them off so no one would know what she was about to do, but she didn't realize that Baxter installed cameras of his own.

This confirmed to Zia that Jazmine knew what was going to happen that night. Jazmine used Zia as bait so she could get to her father. She put Zia's life in danger so she could get revenge and kill Baxter. Jazmine was probably also responsible for Detective John being shot and killed. Jazmine must have kept him out of the loop, so she had a chance to get to Baxter.

Zia was filled with hatred. This wasn't enough to help her now, but it was enough to make her hate Jazmine more than ever before. She'd forgotten about her and how Bryce and Willem were supposed to go see her. She realized they never got the chance. She put the laptop down and left the hotel room. She'd learned everything she could from the folder for now. She needed to find Jazmine and have a few words with her. Zia still thought that she might know something about Baxter's brother and be able to help her.

Jazmine wasn't answering her phone, but as far as Zia knew she still lived in the same place. Zia was able to find a cab even at midnight. She was wary of travelling by herself this late at night, especially since she was still in her tight, short black dress. She was also barefoot and her feet were cold and dirty. She had taken her shoes off at the house before Bryce and Willem were in their accident and had forgotten all about it.

The cab dropped her off in front of Jazmine's building and she gave him the rest of the cash in her purse. The lights were on, so she was sure that someone was home. Zia looked around to make sure there was no one else on the street. She felt like she was being watched, but the events of the night have probably just made her extra paranoid.

She knocked on the door and after a few minutes another light went on downstairs and the door opened. Jazmine was standing on the other side and the moment her eyes fell on Zia, a surprised smile spread across her face, her eyes filled with hatred, and her face contorted into a sick look.

"Well, if it isn't the local backstabbing skank," Jazmine hissed at her. "What the hell do you think you're doing coming here at this time of the night? What the hell are you doing here at all?"

"We need to have a little talk about your fucked-up family," Zia growled and pushed her way past Jazmine into the house.

"My fucked-up family?" Jazmine laughed as she slammed the door closed. "The only one here that's fucked up is you. You backstabbed me, took everything from me, and left me with nothing but my name, and now you want my help."

"You and I both know you deserve everything I did to you. You slept around with my husband behind my back, before and after we got married. You meddled and toyed in my life. You used me as bait just so you can get revenge on your father and kill him. I could have been killed! Detective John was killed! All so you can put two bullets in Baxter's head and take your inheritance."

"You've got it wrong Zee, as usual." Jazmine put her hip out and crossed her arms across her chest. This was her way of taking authority of the situation. She always stood like that when she thought she was in charge. "I never meant for you or Uncle Johnny to get hurt, and Bryce wanted me. I didn't have to do anything but look at him and he begged for my body. I tried to tell you about desire, but you wouldn't listen. It's the most powerful thing in this world. Nothing can beat someone's desire for something."

Zia felt the rage burning inside her. Images of her fists slamming into Jazmine's face and her hands pulling at her hair flashed in her mind. She wanted to rip her to pieces. She needed answers first.

"Who's Alexander," Zia asked.

Jazmine shook her head, "I have no idea, an old boyfriend of yours maybe."

Zia heard the words coming out of Jazmine's mouth, but she watched her eyes instead. They widened when she mentioned the name. She was lying. She knew who Alexander was and Zia realized that she knew to.

"He's your uncle, isn't he?" she said. "Alexander is Baxter's brother."

"What does it matter, geez Zee, you've really lost your mind." Jazmine turned away and started walking up the stairs. "You must have lost that the same night you lost your baby."

"What did you just say?" Zia shouted as her rage took over her body and made her follow Jazmine up the stairs.

They reached the top and Jazmine turned to face her. She had the banister at her back and a long fall below her. She leaned back against it as if she didn't care. Zia stood in front of her leaning forwards and trying to make herself look bigger even though Jazmine was taller than her.

"You know I obviously didn't mean for it to happen," Jazmine continued. "You know how it is when you get angry and all you can think about is getting revenge. Well that was how I felt that night. I found out who that Willem guy was like Bryce said and I gave him a call. That was the easy part. The hard part was following you the rest of the night, turning the power off just before you got in the elevator, and rushing back up the stairs before you could see me." Jazmine laughed like an old lady telling a funny story to her grandchildren. "I think I already proved how much I wanted what my father had, and what I was willing to do to keep it." Jazmine's face turned hard and she looked straight at Zia with emotionless eyes. "My only regret was that I didn't check if you were dead before I left."

She burst out laughing and the next moment was a blur for Zia. She didn't know how it happened, all she knew was that she did it, and that she wanted to do it. She threw her hands out in front of her. They slammed into Jazmine's chest and her laughter was replaced by a sound kind of like gasping for air. Wide eyes filled with fear and a confused look replaced her smug, pleased-with-herself smile.

That was all Zia needed to do. She pushed Jazmine and she stumbled backwards into the banister behind her. Her body's momentum flipped her over the banister and she fell over. It wasn't a long fall but Jazmine was going down head first. Zia didn't run to grab her or look over to watch. She heard Jazmine's head hit the floor below, a loud cracking sound, and then the rest of her body slammed into the ground.

She was frozen in place as her mind tried to catch up with the events her hands just put in place. She took a deep breath and started her climb down the stairs. She got to the bottom and glanced over at Jazmine. Her eyes were wide open but empty and her neck twisted in an unnatural way. Zia didn't need to go to her to check. She was dead. The biggest knot formed in Zia's stomach and it threatened to push everything Zia had eaten that day back up and onto the floor. Zia forced it down. She didn't need there to be any evidence that she was here.

She left the house so quickly that she didn't even think to call a cab. She left the door wide open and ran as far away from the house as fast as she could. She recalled the events of the whole night in her head as she ran. How could all of it make her do this? How could she have so easily thrust her arms out at Jazmine, knowing full well that she would fall over the banister? Zia wasn't about to kid herself. She knew exactly what she was doing in that moment. She didn't just push Jazmine out of frustration, she pushed her because she wanted her to fall over. She wanted to kill her. She convinced herself that Jazmine deserved it.

Zia stopped running after she realized she was in a part of the city that she didn't recognize. The street lights were dim but she was thankful that they were on at all. She glanced at the time on her phone. It was two in the morning. Either her visit to Jazmine's house lasted longer than she thought, or she had been running for at least an hour.

She sat down at the edge of the pavement to catch her breath. It was really dark around her and there were so many alleyways and shadows that could be hiding an attacker. She wasn't bothered by that now. She got sidetracked at Jazmine's house, but she still got something out of it. Judging by Jazmine's reaction when she mentioned Alexander's name, she was sure he was Baxter's brother and the stalker doing all of this to her.

She knows that for some reason he was recently in a psychiatric institute and Baxter had to check him out of it. There had to be a reason why he was in there. Zia didn't have time to go to New York and visit the institute herself. She needed a way to ask them questions about Alexander. She couldn't head into war with him without knowing who he was and what he was capable of.

She decided to research the institute on her phone and she found an emergency number to call. She doubted anyone would answer at this time of night. She dialed the number anyway, hoping that there was at least a graveyard shift to answer her call. The phone rang for a while and Zia was about to give up hope when someone picked it up on the other end.

"New York City Psychiatric Institute," the voice wasn't robotic, so it wasn't an answering machine, but it seemed tired and uninterested in the conversation to come.

"Hi there," Zia put on her best phone voice. "I was hoping you could help me find some information about one of your past patients. His name is Alexander Fairfield." Zia hoped that he shared the same name as Dwight.

"I'm sorry ma'am but we can't just hand out information like that unless you're a family member."

Zia cursed under her breath, she wasn't surprised but she hoped they would be too tired to argue with her. She had to think of something fast. Any lie she was about to tell would be discredited by the long silence that came before it.

"Oh, but I am family," she blurted out. "I'm his brother's wife, Dwight Fairfield. You see Dwight checked his brother out of the institute and unfortunately he disappeared not long after that. Tragically Dwight died and I'm just trying to track down family members so I can sort out his will." Zia wasn't surprised by how easily the lie came out of her mouth. She'd done far worse than lie tonight. Her entire life was at stake and she was willing to do anything to save it.

"Alright," the person on the other end sighed. "Please give me a moment ma'am," the line went silent for a moment, but Zia was sure she heard them mutter, "It's too late for this shit," before it went silent for good.

She waited patiently with the phone pressed tight to her ear and her eyes glancing around constantly. She felt like a sitting duck on the hunting grounds. There was a chill in the air that should have made her shiver, but she was too busy to worry about how cold it is. After a while she heard some movement on the phone and the person picked it back up.

"Hello ma'am, are you still there?"

"Yes, I'm here," Zia sounded more excited than she was meaning to. "Did you find something?"

"Alexander Fairfield stayed with us for about 8 years. He was checked in by his mother and a police officer and then checked back out 8 years later by his brother and a Detective John. We have no records of him after that point, so I'm afraid we can't tell you where he is now."

Zia took in all the information, but it just confused her more. Why would his mother need a police officer to check him into a psychiatric institute and why would Dwight need Detective John to check him out. Up until now she'd assumed Detective John knew nothing about Baxter's brother, but it turns out he did.

Zia sighed, now for the hard part.

"Do you by any chance know why he was in the institute in the first place? I think it's important for me to know before I go looking for him you know. Just to be safe." Zia kept her fingers crossed that was enough of an excuse.

"Well, I'm not actually supposed to give you this information, but I guess you do have a point." They sighed and Zia heard them flipping through pages. "It says here that Alexander Fairfield was sentenced to a stay at the institute by a judge's ruling. His mother was to be accompanied by a police officer and both their signatures were needed to check him in. Then both a family member's signature and a police officer's signature, or someone ranking higher, was needed to check him out again. Only once it was determined by a doctor that his treatment was complete, and he was ready to rejoin society could he be checked out of the hospital."

"Wow," Zia breathed. "That sounds really serious. Did he do something bad? Dwight never really talked about his family much, so this is my first time realizing he even had a brother."

"Oh, I understand," she seemed like a nice lady. In another life Zia might have been friends with her. "It says here that he was arrested and convicted of murder, but he was sent here instead of jail because the court found that he was not mentally stable or aware of his actions at the time. Oh my! It says he killed his father by pushing him into an industrial wood chipper! Oh my god! Ma'am, I would suggest you not look for him at all. It says here that he wasn't deemed safe to rejoin society by a doctor."

Zia gasped and her stomach knotted up once again.

"How is that possible?"

"I'm not sure, but it says here that he wasn't finished with his treatment and that he shouldn't have been checked out. I'm not sure why he was allowed to leave ma'am. I suggest you stay as far away from him as possible. Ma'am, are you still there?"

Zia didn't know what to say. Her voice had been stolen by fear and it wasn't giving it back. Her breathing was heavy and with each breath she took, the colder she got. It felt like her Bone were frozen.

"Thank you for your help," Zia finally managed to say before hanging up.

Now she knew who he was and what he was capable of. She already knew he was capable of kidnapping and murdering people. She never imagined that he'd been doing it since he was a child. He killed his own father and that takes a certain kind of madness to do. Zia wasn't afraid though. She was ready for him and whatever he had planned for her. Alexander might be a killer and willing to take everything away from her and burn her life to the ground, but that didn't matter because Zia was a killer too and she was willing to do whatever it took to save her family.

ZIA DID SOMETHING SHE NEVER THOUGHT SHE WOULD do. She searched her phone for the unknown number that had called her earlier in the night and she called it back. She stood up and started walking while she waited for Alexander to answer the call. He did answer and even though her heart jumped into her throat, she maintained her composure and spoke calmly.

"Hello Alexander," she said.

"Zia? I am impressed, but I knew you would come to me eventually." His voice was so confident Zia could just see the smile on his face. "Are you ready to take your place as my queen?"

"I'm ready for you, but not in the way you think," Zia tried to mimic the confidence in his voice. "I'm coming to get my parents back, Alexander, and you're going to give them to me. You've made your point and I won't let you hurt anyone else I love."

"Oh, I assume you found out that your husband and lover got into an accident. That's a little trick I learned from my dear brother, he taught me a lot of things. It's such a shame that they weren't going fast enough for the crash to kill them."

Zia clenched her fists and tightened her jaw. She managed to find her way to a main road and it was busy. She stood at the side of the road and waited for a cab to drive by.

"You're a monster and you'll never be anything like your brother," she growled at him. "He might have had some crazy ideas and he might have killed people, but he still loved me in some way. I don't think you even know what love is."

"You've got me there," he chuckled, "but it is hard to know what something is if you've never been shown it before. How about we stop playing games with each other and put an end to this cat and mouse."

"I supposed you think you're the cat, huh?" A cab drove up and Zia managed to flag it down. "Alright then, how do you want to do this?"

"How about we finish this where it all started? Meet me in the basement of Fargo Tower, come alone or mommy and daddy will be saying hi to your stupid dog for you."

Zia wanted to be the one to hang up, but Alexander beat her to it. She put the phone down and got into the cab. She instructed the driver where to go and kept the fact that she had no money on her to herself. Once she got to the destination there wasn't much the cab driver could do to her if she didn't pay.

During the drive she thought about a lot of things. She thought about Bryce lying unconscious in a hospital bed and how it was her fault he was there. She thought about Willem and how he knew more about Baxter than he was letting on. She wasn't willing to trust him ever again now. He was hiding something from her. She thought about calling the police to meet her there, but then the image of her parents lying dead on the floor flashed past her eyes. If she called the police, Alexander would kill them, disappear into the night, and then this would all start over again. She needed to end it now and she needed to do it alone.

She spotted Fargo Tower looming in the distance. She never thought she would come back here again, at least not in real life. She'd visited this place in her dreams and in her memories, but those were safe. This was dangerous but she had no choice. They arrived and Zia faked searching through her purse for some money. She informed the driver that she didn't have any and he proceeded to swear at her and call her all sorts of foul names before kicking her out of the cab. That was easier than Zia thought it would be. She climbed out of the cab and walked up to the building while the cab drove away.

As she neared the main entrance, she realized that she would have to break in. Then she spotted a piece of paper taped to the glass door with an arrow pointing down. Below it, lying on the ground was a keycard for the building. She leaned down and picked it up. It was her old keycard from when she used to work at Spark. She doubted it would still open the doors but then she reminded herself how smart Alexander is. She tried the key card and the door unlocked for her.

As Zia walked into the building, she imagined that Alexander had been planning this meeting for a long time. She wondered where he got her keycard from and how long he'd been holding onto it. How long has he wanted to bring her back here? How long has he been waiting to relive the night that Baxter was killed?

The building always looked different at night than it did during the day, but Zia felt that tonight it looked even more sinister than it ever had. The walls seemed to move and whisper. The shadows hid monstrous faces that hissed and snarled at her. She could see glowing eyes in the darkness, hungry for her, and stalking her.

Her bare feet allowed her to move through the building silently, but her tight dress forced her to move slowly. She peeked around every corner, glanced behind her shoulder constantly, and kept her fists at the ready. She wouldn't let someone sneak up on her. She was ready to fight her way out of this.

Zia made her way down to the utility room. That was where it started back when Baxter took her down there. That was where she would find her parents, and possibly Alexander. She knew it was a trap and he was probably waiting for her. She was fully aware that she was about to walk full steam into his trap. She was also aware that she had no choice. Her parents and Bryce were counting on her to see this through and finish what Jazmine started when she killed Baxter.

Zia tried to stay detached from the situation but as she walked through the building, she wasn't able to keep the memories of that night from forcing their way into her mind. She saw the spot where Baxter had died and where Detective John had died. Instead of seeing a clean floor, she saw puddles of blood. She hurried the rest of the way to the utility room.

She tried the door, but it was locked. She put her ear up to the door and she could hear muffled sounds on the other side. Zia banged on the door hoping that someone would open it up. She knew someone was in there. She had a feeling it was just her parents and Alexander was somewhere else.

Her phone rang and she nearly jumped out of her skin. She didn't hesitate to answer it.

"You didn't think it would be that easy," Alexander's confident and annoying voice floated through the speaker.

"I thought you said you were done playing games," Zia kept trying to open the door while she talked. Her parents were in there, she knew it.

"Perhaps we have time to play one more game. I'm the cat and you're the mouse, you have to run away from me and I have to chase you. If I catch you … well, you know what happens when a cat catches a mouse, don't you?"

Zia swallowed the lump forming in her throat.

"I'm not going to play your sick games, Alexander!"

"My dear queen, I'm afraid you have no choice." There was a loud sound, like something powering up, and all of the lights in the building turned on. Zia had to squint to avoid going blind. "Let the games begin."

The line went dead and Zia put her phone in her purse then placed it on the floor. She tried the door a few more times but she wasn't strong enough to break it open. She needed the key or a tool of some kind. For now, she needed to turn the power off so she could play this stupid game of his. With the lights on he could find her easier. If he wanted to play games with her then she would play his game and play it better.

She left her purse by the door and made her way back through the building. There was no point being sneaky with all the lights on. Wherever Alexander is, he could see her no matter what. She was like an ant underneath a magnifying glass.

She ran through the long hallways and headed straight for the security room. That's where she can turn the power off again. She expected Alexander to jump out at her at any moment, but she didn't let that slow her down. She reached the security room and snuck in. It was empty. She glanced at the security cameras but they were off so she won't be finding Alexander that way.

She made her way to the back of the room where the power switches were. She was thankful for the tour she took when that one security guard had a thing for her. He showed her everything she needed to know for this moment. She wasn't sure which switch would turn the power off, so she flipped all of the switches at once. There was another loud mechanical sound and everything powered down. Zia had turned off all the power to the building, the lights, the power to the doors and elevators, and even the security cameras.

It was pitch black but she didn't care. This was the first step to her winning Alexander's game. She thought that he might come down here and turn it back on again. She searched the room for something she could use to damage the switch board. There was a cup filled with liquid on the security desk. She picked it up and threw it on the switch board. Sparks flew through the air which made Zia jump back and drop the cup. She smiled to herself and made her way for the door.

"Zia! Is that you in there?" Alexander's voice echoed down the hallway and floated in through the open door.

Zia gasped and dropped to the ground. She could barely see anything in the room but she knew that Alexander would be able to see her if she didn't hide. She crawled on her hands and knees to the security desk and hid underneath it just as she heard Alexander's footsteps enter the room.

"Tisk, tisk, tisk, Zia," he spoke as he took slow steps through the room. "I never pegged you for the cheating kind."

She watched his feet from underneath the desk move across the room. He reached the switch board and tried to flip one of the switches. At first nothing happened and then a spark shot out and electrocuted his fingers. He jumped back and cursed under his breath.

"Okay Zia, if that's the way you want to play," he called out loudly. She thought that perhaps he didn't know she was here anymore. "I'm coming for you little mouse."

She held her breath as he walked past her again and left the room. She stayed underneath the desk for a while longer. She stayed there even after his footsteps faded down the hall. Only when she was certain that he was gone did she crawl out from underneath the desk.

She sat on the ground for a moment as she thought of her next move. She needed to get her parents out of here. To do that she needed to open that door. She thought that maybe the security guards would have the key to the door. She got up and began searching the room as quietly as she could. She used her hands to feel for any keys hanging on the walls. She didn't find any. She then went to the desk and started searching through the drawers. She finally found a large ring with more than 20 keys on it. One of them has to be the key she needs, so she took all of them and left the room.

She'd never felt so sneaky in her entire life. She walked slowly and stayed on her tiptoes so she made the least amount of noise possible. She got down on her knees and glanced around corners before taking them. She pressed up against the wall in a large hallway and hoped she blended in with the wallpaper. She was thankful to be wearing a black dress. That helped her blend in with the shadows. On her way to the utility room, she heard Alexander's footsteps somewhere above her. She got down on her knees and continued to crawl past him, hoping he wouldn't see or hear her.

She made it to the utility room and started trying all of the keys. She was surprised that Alexander didn't come here to meet her. He must not have thought that she would try and rescue her parents. Unless he truly believed that she wanted to play this game of his. He must think that she's as mad as him.

It didn't take her long to find the right key and she unlocked the door. She opened the door slowly and hoped it wouldn't make a noise to alert Alexander. It was so quiet that the slightest sound would echo through the building. She opened the door wide enough for her to squeeze through. Then she grabbed her purse and closed the door behind her. She searched for her phone and then used the illuminated screen to see in the pitch black room.

The light shone on her parents huddled in the back corner of the room. Their hands and feet were bound with duct tape and their faces were badly bruised. Their eyes were wide but filled with relief when they saw her.

"Mom! Dad!" Zia rushed to them. She hugged them both and then examined the duct tape. "Don't worry, I'm going to get you out of this."

She immediately started searching the room for something she could use. It was the utility room, so it was basically filled with weapons and objects that could help her out of this situation. She found a pair of scissors and cut through their bonds. Then she untied the clothes around their mouths and pulled them away.

Zia's mother burst into tears and they both opened their mouths to speak but Zia didn't let them.

"We don't have a lot of time," she told them. "Sooner or later he'll come down here looking for me. We need to get out of the building. We need to do it fast and silently. He can't catch us."

Zia's parents had so many questions to ask but they just nodded and followed their daughter as she led the way. Before leaving the room, Zia found a large wrench lying on the floor by the door. She picked it up and took it with her. Her parents stayed close to her as she made her way to the front of the building. She could see the exit ahead of her and the moonlight flooding through. She picked up the pace until she and her parents were running toward the exit. She could taste freedom in her throat and it made her smile. As soon as the smile appeared on her face it faded away.

"What do you think you're doing, Zia?" She heard Alexander yell from behind them. They all spun around to see Alexander standing on an overhanging walkway looking down at them. "This isn't how you play the game Zia!"

Zia wasn't sure what to do. If she and her parents ran out of the building, he would follow them and her parents might get caught, or worse. She needed to give them a chance to escape.

"Run!" She yelled to them and started running the opposite way. "Run, get out of here!"

She ran back into the building and Alexander followed her. She didn't know if her parents listened to her, but all she needed to know was that Alexander was following her and not them.

She ran through the halls and tried her best to zig-zag through the building. She needed to lose him and then escape somehow. She held the wrench tightly in her hand and was prepared to swing it at anything or anyone that came to close. She found a set of stairs and ran up them. He was close behind her. She could hear his footsteps slamming on the tiles and gaining on her. She reached the elevator but it was a dead end and the power was off so she couldn't use them to escape. Alexander was right behind her, so she turned to face him. Her wrench was hidden behind her back and held tightly in her grip.

She finally set her sights on Alexander for the first time. She couldn't believe her eyes but she knew it was true. It was him. He looked like Baxter. He was shorter and not as muscular, but it was him. He had Baxter's eyes, his hair, and his smile. She was looking at Baxter's face but she knew it wasn't Baxter.

"Little mouse caught in a trap she set for herself, whatever will she do?" His smile was sickening. He walked toward her slowly. "Zia, my queen, this will be so much easier if you just accept your fate. You were born to rule beside me, and I was born to cleanse this world of the filth upon it."

Zia backed away until her spine hit the cold elevator doors. There was no other way out of this. She had to face him head on.

"I thought it was Dwight's destiny to be the king and I would be his queen?" She needed to keep him talking and make him trust her, just like she did with Baxter.

"My brother set out on that course but he failed because he got too close. He taught me everything he knew and now it is my turn to carry the gauntlet he dropped over the finish line." He kept walking towards her, his smile growing large and showing more teeth with every word he spoke. "Thank you for dealing with Jazmine by the way. She was going to be my next stop after this, but now I don't need to bother. All the loose ends are tied, and everything is right again. All that's left now is to take my queen away from this place."

He was only inches away from her now and he reached out to grab her face. Zia swung the wrench at his head and slammed it across his face. He cried out and stumbled backwards. He cradled his face as blood dripped to the floor. She tried to push past him and run away but he recovered quickly. He grabbed her wrist and pulled her back. She lifted the wrench for a second time but he caught her wrist in the air before she could hit him with it.

They struggled as she attempted to pull one of her arms free, but he held them tight and squeezed. She cried out at the pain but kept her eye on the prize. She leaned forward and dug her teeth into his fingers. Blood trickled down her throat and she wanted to spit it out but she kept digging her teeth into his flesh. He eventually pulled his hand away from her, freeing one of her arms. She used her free arm to punch him in the face. He staggered backwards and let go of her other arm. She swung the wrench at him again, this time hitting the other side of his face. This hit was hard enough to send him to the ground.

Blood was pouring out of his fingers and from both gashes in his head. He pushed himself up onto his hands and knees and took a moment to catch his breath.

"You stupid bitch!" He shouted out but it came out strange and didn't sound like it should have. Zia figured that she might have broken his jaw and a few teeth. "You were going to be my queen! Now you're as good as dead."

Zia stood over him with the wrench at the ready. She used both arms to raise it high above her head.

"You're smart Alexander, but you made one mistake," she gasped as she spoke. "This one mistake is what broke you down and put you in this position."

He glanced over his shoulder and looked up at her.

"What mistake is that?" Blood splattered out of his mouth when he spoke.

Zia smiled a devilish smile.

"You thought I was the mouse, but I'm the cat."

She used all the strength she had left in her to bring the wrench down. One last blow to the back of the head was all she needed. His body collapsed, blood pooled on the floor beneath him and he coughed a few times before falling silent and lifeless. Zia dropped the wrench on the ground and walked away. It was over. She was finally free from the nightmare that had plagued her life ever since she decided to read a book called Chiseled Bone.

COMING SOON

CayellePublishing.com

amazon.com

MORE READS

CayellePublishing.com

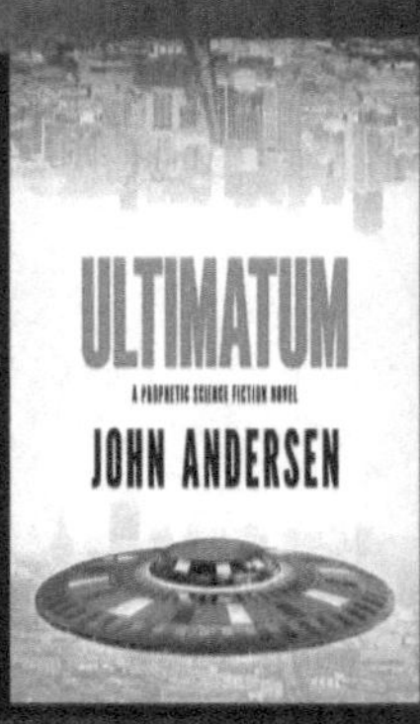

amazon.com

COMING SOON

CayellePublishing.com

amazon.com

CayéllePublishing.com

www.ingramcontent.com/pod-product-compliance
Lightning Source LLC
Chambersburg PA
CBHW030757200726
48288CB00004B/1214